NEMROZ
THE
PRIEST

NEMROZ

THE

PRIEST

PART 1

EXONA MOLL

1603 Capitol Ave., Suite 310 Cheyenne, Wyoming USA 82001
1-888-980-6523 | admin@urlinkpublishing.com

URLink Print and Media is committed to excellence in the publishing industry.

Book design copyright © 2022 by URLink Print and Media. All rights reserved.

Published in the United States of America

Library of Congress Control Number: 2022904842
ISBN 978-1-68486-139-2 (Paperback)
ISBN 978-1-68486-140-8 (Digital)

11.03.22

CHAPTER

1

Very many years ago in a far off land there was a pagan temple for the worship of a god called 'Farago'. He was a god of fertility, that the people went to when having trouble with conceiving. The 'treatment' was administered by the priests of the temple. The recipience mostly had no idea what was involved in providing the 'treatment'.

In the business parts of the temple, things were very different. The public part of the temple was very grand, dominated by a huge statue of Farago and the altar that was attached. The area where the priests lived and worked and further back still where the sacrifices where bred were unseen.

The hub of the temple was the High Priest, who's highly ritualized life was spent permanently in his chambers behind the altar. Some years before, the High Priest who lived there had become a legend. And the model for all High Priests who came after him.

The new High Priest was usually chosen by election by the senior priests, who ran the administration. Then at his investiture he was taken to the chambers and only the electors were present. His robes were removed. He would never again be clothed, except when he was required to go to the outer chambers. When he was covered by a wonderfully decorated cloak. Almost all his time was spent in the main chamber or his sleeping chamber, and in both he was totally naked.

Unrevealed to the recipience was the process of sacrificing mostly young women, or even girls to the god Farago, to yield the blood that was used in the 'treatment'.

In the women's quarters at the back of the temple, pregnant slaves or sometimes even unmarried mothers or rape victims were brought to give birth. If the babies were girls they were brought up to be used as 'offerings'. When they were old enough they were brought to the High Priest to be prepared and sanctified. Two young priests would bring the unfortunate girl and present her to the High Priest. They were brought six chalices, two of milk, two of wine and two of water. The High Priest would explain that the milk was Farago's provision to them, they drank one each. The wine was their sanctification, and the water was their suffering. At each stage they both drained the chalices. Then it was the High Priest's duty to explain the Farago would penetrate her and accept the offering of her life, and what an honour that was. It had become practise that as Farago's human representative he would demonstrate. But if he got carried away and 'entered her as a man' as it was referred to as, he would pay with his own life. So the level of control that was required and the stress that coursed was immense.

The legendary High Priest was able to maintain that for years, and yet he was kind to both the 'offering' and the young priests who served him, and everyone adored him.

CHAPTER

2

Our story really begins with the investiture of the latest High Priest. All investitures now took the form of that legendary High Priest. Our priest was called Zormen. He was proud he had been chosen and thought he had the control to cope. In many ways he was much like his hero. At first he was coping well and he was very popular, even among the older priests.

One day one of them asked him if he wanted to see the crypt. The most famous High Priests had been mummified, and they were kept in the crypt. It was a rare honour to be taken down to the crypt, even for a High Priest. It was Zormen's ambition to be mummified one day.

He had been High Priest for nearly ten years. Few of his predecessors in later times had lasted as long as that. The strain was beginning to tell.

One day a young woman was brought to him who he had real feelings for, and the prospect of what she would have to endure when she left him, was beginning to torture him. The previous lass was lasting longer than usual, (I think I have not explained the training lasted for the length of time it took the previous 'offering' to surrender/ die). By the time he was called to perform the final duty, which was the final ritual for the 'offering' when she was taken down from the altar, and the sanctifying of the next. The stress broke him. The young priests had to restrain him, for them to take his 'offering'.

Zormen had many friends in the main priesthood. When they heard the commotion many of them came to his aid, but not in time to rescue his lady before the penetration. They lifted her down, but she was already bleeding. They tried to staunch the bleeding, but that caused her terrible agony. A crazed Zormen broke free and rushed to her side. His friends managed to smuggle them out of the temple. There were many rumours about what happened to them. But no one knew for sure.

CHAPTER

3

The whole temple was in an uproar. There was one priest slightly older than Zormen's young friends. He was an imposing man, in both his character and his physic. He took charge and made himself High Priest. He restored order to the temple by force. But he was very unpopular. He reinstated the ritual of the 'offerings' with the first one not going through the process of sanctification. The poor child was just hauled straight up on the altar. He claimed it was his right to enter the 'offerings' just as he liked and as often as he liked. It was a nightmare for the poor girls. And no one dared stop him, or they finished up on the altar themselves.

The young priests were plotting to find a way to overthrow him. They had chosen a priest called Roz to be their leader. But the gods intervened. The brute had not been High Priest for long when, one day he was entering an 'offering' 'as a man', as was his way, when he dropped dead. (It was probably a heart attack, but they did not know about such things in those days.)

The young priests took over and invested Roz as High Priest. Many priests took a new name when they were invested. Roz claimed the name of his hero. But he said he was not worthy to be called Zormen, so he changed it to Nemroz.

Nemroz was a reluctant High Priest, he said he was not worthy and he was not trained. There were still some assistants who had served under Zormen. They helped teach Nemroz the rituals that were expected of him.

Nemroz started his duties in his new quarters straight away after his investiture. But he insisted that none of the girls were thrown straight on the altar. It was hard, especially at first when he himself was unsure of how the details worked as it was only the High Priest himself, and to a certain extent his assistants that knew in detail, what was done. Normally the retiring High Priest would train his successor.

After only a few days the first young 'offering' was sent through to the priests in charge of the altar itself. So it was not until the second 'offering' arrived that the full ritual came into force.

Nemroz had not realized before his investiture the extent of the control that was going to be asked of him. Partly because he had never experienced that sensation before.

All he had during the day was the ritual cups he had with the 'offerings'. Then just had a meal in the evening, which he had in his sleeping chamber, as the 'offering' was not allowed any.

His dear friend Polto had largely been responsible for getting Nemroz voted as the leader of their group and later as the new High Priest. When he came to hear that Nemroz was struggling with his duties, he felt very guilty. He felt he should help. He decided he would send his close friend Darius to help.

He suggested to Darius that he would send him to Nemroz, Darius was sad. But he felt it was a great honour to surrender himself for the use of the High Priest.

Polto was not able to contact Nemroz direct, so he just took Darius to the High Priest's quarters and explained to the priest assistant on guard duty at the chamber door that Darius was to be taken to the High Priest's bed chamber. After a brief goodbye they parted. Darius was taken through the door, from which he would never be allowed to return.

The priest assistant took him through to the sleeping chamber. Nemroz was in the main chamber with the 'offering' and he was curious what was going on. As soon as he was free, he followed the two visitors into the sleeping chamber. He stopped on entering asking what was going on.

The priest assistant said, "You have been given a present."

Nemroz looked puzzled.

"This young man has been given to you as a present. He is to be a comfort and a help for you." Then he added sarcastically, "When your duties are difficult."

Nemroz and Darius stood looking at each other.

The priest continued, looking straight at Darius, "You are to surrender to the High Priest." When Darius did not move, he continued abruptly, "Remove your robes."

Not sure what was happening Darius did as he was told.

The priest took all the clothes and said, "You now belong to the High Priest, you are to do anything he tells you."

The priest turned and left. Nemroz and Darius continued standing in silence, looking at each other, wondering what had happened. Poor Darius was looking scared, Nemroz pulled himself together and said, "It is alright I will not harm you. Please tell me what has just happened."

"Polto somehow learned you were struggling, he was not in the position to send you a female body. He knew a male would be acceptable, so he sent me."

Nemroz replied, "Who are you? I do not understand."

"When you are preforming your duties, you wish to enter your charge 'as a man', but that would mean for you a painful, dishonourable death."

"Who are you? You know too much."

"I am Darius, a junior member of your group."

"Why would Polto send you?"

"I am a very close friend of Polto's. He knows I would do anything for him and I can be the nearest thing to a woman for you." Nemroz still looked puzzled so Darius continued, "How well do you know Polto?"

Nemroz replied, "We have been friends since we were toddlers in the women's quarters."

"Do you know Polto desires you as most men desire a woman?"

Nemroz looked shocked, but he replied, "Do you desire me?"

"No I desire Polto." Darius suddenly looked bashful. "I should not be speaking to my master like this."

"It is alright, I asked you to. It was good of you to tell me."

There were tears in Darius's eyes as he fell at Nemroz's feet.

Nemroz responded, "I appreciate your deference, but please rise."

Darius stood and shyly asked, "What should I call you?"

Nemroz mused, "The priests call me your godliness, but please do not call me that. My name would not be appropriate. Perhaps sir, or my master."

Darius looked away shyly and asked, "Can I sit with you sir?"

"Of course you can." He went and sat on his couch and indicated for Darius to sit beside him.

It was not long before there was a knock on the door. Nemroz rose and answered it. It was the priest assistant saying it was time for him to join his 'offering'

Nemroz replied, "I will join you in a moment." And closed the door.

Returning to Darius, he explained that Darius would not be able to join them.

"I eat in the evening, I will arrange for the priest to bring two meals."

Nemroz gave no further explanation, and left the chamber. Darius waited quietly for his master to return.

Nemroz went through the usual ritual with his young charge, and as was often the case, she was particularly reluctant to drain the chalice of water. But after repeating the situation with his own case, she did as asked, (He had explained that one day, when his ministry was over, he would himself be offered on the altar.)

It was Nemroz's duty to explain to the 'offering' what was going to be expected of her. When asked if she was clear now as to the procedure, she said she was. So, he thanked her and told her he would return in the morning. He then returned to his chamber.

Darius smiled with great pleasure as he entered the chamber, he closed the door behind him. He ran to greet him, asking if he was okay. Nemroz grinned appreciatively saying, "We only shared the ritual chalices, so it was not stressful."

When Darius seemed unsure what he should be doing, Nemroz added, "Just sit with me for now, I have arranged for a meal for you as well. It should be here soon.

When it arrived Nemroz asked the priest if he had found the extra chair he had asked for.

He answered, rather irritably. "Not yet your godliness." He placed the plates on the table grumbling, "He could not carry everything at once if he was to bring two meals."

When he had left Darius said, "That is fine, I can have my plate on my lap. It is kind of you to arrange for me to have a meal brought."

The priest returned with two beakers of water saying, "I will try to find a chair tomorrow."

They ate their meal in silence.

When they had finished and the priest assistant had collected the plates, Nemroz joined Darius on the couch. They just lay together all night. For Nemroz the company was a great comfort. When they woke next morning he gazed at Darius saying, "I hope no one takes you from me."

Darius through his arms around him, just grateful to be wanted. Nemroz explained he was called early to share the chalices with the 'offering'. He was so sad that Darius was not to join them, but Darius was doomed (as they thought) to spend the rest of his life in the sleeping chamber.

Soon the knock came on the door, and Nemroz had to leave. The 'offering' seemed more co-operative this time. When she had drained all three chalices she asked, "Can you show me again how Farago will come to me?"

A little taken aback by her sudden boldness, Nemroz lifted her onto the couch, but it was rather unexpected and he was not ready at first. But soon he managed.

He gently slid into her and lay quite still, intending to draw straight out. But his charge gripped him with her legs and responded to him. Nemroz was struggling desperately to control the situation. He managed to break free and rushed to his chamber.

He quickly closed the door behind him and leaned his back against it. Darius rushed to his side and Nemroz panted, "I need you, I need you!"

Darius took him by the hand and laid himself ready for Nemroz.

When Nemroz had satisfied himself, he rolled Darius over to face him, saying how grateful he was to him and to Polto for sending Darius to him. They remained on the couch, talking quietly until the knock on the door came again.

Nemroz was not surprised when he was asked to explain what had happened at the morning ritual. The assistant seemed satisfied with the explanation. Nemroz made sure that time that it was only the chalices. But his charge had many questions. He stayed a while to ease her fears and her loneliness for at least a short time. With his first few charges he had spent much of his time with them, but now he had Darius to consider as well.

When one of the friendly assistants who had helped him at first was on duty, he asked if the assistant could sit with the girls. He agreed that when he was on duty he would, but he didn't know whether the others would.

When Nemroz returned to his chamber he was anxious to talk to Darius who was still on the edge of the couch.

"I am so sorry I cannot spend more time with you."

"My dear master, do not worry about me, you have your own difficulties to deal with."

"But I cannot expect you to sit here on your own all day with nothing to do."

"It is just marvellous to know I am wanted."

"I am sorry I will need to go to the 'offering' again before it is time for the meal. Then after that we can be together. We can talk about it then."

"I am impressed you care."

Again there was a knock at the door, and Nemroz left.

He did not stay so long this time. Soon after he returned two priests assistants carrying a meal each, entered the chamber. They still had not brought a chair. Nemroz moved the table so that Darius could sit on the couch and reach the table.

When they had finished and a priest had taken the plates, they sat together on the couch.

Nemroz started, "When you were one of the young priests and you were off duty. What kind of things did you do?"

"The other lads used to play games, but they never let me join in."

Nemroz through his arms around him, not knowing how to continue.

Then after a while he added, "We must find something for you to do. Being isolated here on your own with nothing to do, is not right."

All Darius said was, "My master is very kind."

The next day started ordinarily enough. Nemroz preformed the usual ritual meal, but he avoided physical contact, returning to his chamber straight afterwards. Soon after that there was a commotion in the main chamber. One of the priest assistants came to inform Nemroz what was going on. But he glared at Darius.

Nemroz intervened, saying, "Anything you have to say to me can be said in front of my helper."

After a hard disapproving look he started, "A fallen priest has been caught in the act. There is no need for a trial. As I said he was caught in the act. We will not need you to attend at the moment, unless you want to. But we will need you to administer the punishment before he is taken to Farago. You will continue with your other duties until Farago is ready for this 'offering'" Then he turned and left.

Darius sat in silence, looking at Nemroz in horror. At last he said, "I was not sure this actually happened."

Nemroz replied, "Oh it happens and I have to do it."

Nemroz had gone very pale, so Darius did not say any more.

When Nemroz did not move, or say another word, Darius said, "Can I help?"

"No not really." Then added, "When the time comes I will say you are coming too. Will you cope with that?"

"I thought I could never leave this chamber."

"You, like me, can never leave these quarters, but if I say you are to leave this chamber, that is for me to say. I need you beside me.."

Darius looked frightened, but he fell at Nemroz's feet saying, "I am yours to command."

"Yes, but I want you to agree."

"Yes of course I agree."

Soon it was time for Nemroz to minister to his charge again.

He turned to Darius and said, "I wish I could share the ritual meals with you, but I have no control over that."

Darius was so choked with emotion, he could not reply.

The rest of the day and all of the next continued as normal. Then during the following day the call came for Nemroz to attend the small chamber.

Nemroz went white saying, "I will join you in a moment."

As soon as the door was shut he rushed to Darius saying, "Help me!" Pulling Darius' hands to his private parts. Darius found it hard to arouse him at first. But as Nemroz relaxed to Darius' touch he came. With a look of almost desperation, he left.

Nemroz went with the priest assistant to the small chamber to perform the duty he hated most. He had to 'sanctify' the bloodstained corpse of the last 'offering' ready to 'consecrate' the one waiting in the main chamber. (It was the one time he was expected to go all the way, but that was very difficult). His whole front spattered with blood, he must have looked a terrifying sight. He then transferred the blood to the next 'offering', before he could return to his chamber to clean up.

Darius waited anxiously for Nemroz to return. As soon as he entered Darius rushed to fetch some water to help Nemroz clean himself. While Darius emptied the water away Nemroz collapsed onto the couch.

Life for the pair of them was very different for the next few days. There was no new 'offering' waiting in the main chamber. Nemroz had never been involved in the process in the punishment cell. That evening they were informed they were on a fast until the punishment process was over. From then on all they were brought was water. But it did give them more time to themselves, to sort out how they would deal with the situation Darius was in.

Nemroz said again that Darius was not to be expected to be isolated and alone, day after day with nothing to do. But Darius himself could see no solution to the problem.

At least for the three days they were isolated together. On the fourth day, late afternoon, the call Nemroz had been dreading, came. He was to go to the small chamber. Nemroz proved to be correct in assuming he would be expected to go straight to the punishment cell as soon as he had preformed his duty in the small chamber.

He stated firmly, he would come in a moment.

As soon as the door was shut he turned to Darius. Before he was even asked he stepped forward to help arouse Nemroz. Then when he succeeded Nemroz asked, "Will you come with me?"

Darius walked towards the door and held out his hand to Nemroz. They walked first to the small chamber. Darius was very pale and silent as he followed Nemroz into the chamber.

On the floor lay the bloodstained corpse of the young 'offering'. Darius turned away feeling sick, as Nemroz preformed his duty. Then when he had finished the assistant did not even allow him to go to clean up. They were to go straight to the punishment cell. In desperation Nemroz held out his hand to Darius. None of the assistants dared to stop him.

As they entered the cell they saw the poor unfortunate young man, naked and chained to the wall, while the girl was shackled to the floor. Two other assistants had been watching over them. One of whom held a very sharp looking blade, with a fancy gold handle. He passed it to Nemroz. Then stooped to the floor and turned the girl's head, for her to see what was happening, saying bluntly, "Watch to see what you have caused your lover."

Nemroz looked pleadingly at Darius. He stepped forward and brought the blade swiftly down on the poor victim's private parts. They were not severed the first time, and Nemroz had to strike again. The victim stood bravely erect. The second assistant came forward with a bowl, in which was a rag tied to a stick. Nemroz cringed and shuddered as he thrust the ball on the young man's wounds. He screamed with agony as the liquid staunched the flow of blood. Nemroz grabbed Darius and ran from the cell, not caring what the assistants thought of him, pulling the door shut with his blood-spattered hands. He through his arms around Darius and ran for the sleeping chamber. He closed the door behind him and leaned back on the door.

He stood sobbing and Darius rushed to the closet and through up. When he had got himself a bit more under control, he returned with a bowl of water and they cleaned each other up. Then Darius poured away the water.

It was not until Darius had returned and they were sitting on the couch together, was Nemroz able to speak.

He sobbed, "I am sorry to put you through that. I could not have done that without someone by my side."

Darius was still too emotional to speak. He just fell on his knees before Nemroz and wept.

It was some time before he rose and sat beside Nemroz again. He looked sadly at him and asked. "What will happen to the young man now?"

Nemroz calmly replied, "He will be taken down, then led out and offered to Farago."

Darius cringed and through his arms around Nemroz. Then he pursued, "And what will happen to that poor girl? And also what will life be like for us?"

Nemroz replied, "The girl will stay where she is until her lover surrenders to Farago, then she will be offered to Farago. But I do not know at that stage whether she will be sanctified by me. But she will not receive the ritual meals."

"Will that mean we are still fasting?"

"I would imagine so."

It was some time before the assistant was ready to bring the beakers of water. And when he did, he was not pleased with the way Nemroz had behaved.

For three days sometimes water arrived. Sometimes it didn't. But at least they were left in peace. Neither of them felt like doing much. Sometimes they talked, but most of the time they just lay together on the couch.

On the morning of the fourth day Nemroz had a call from the priest assistant, asking him to go to the small chamber. Darius asked if he wanted him to come too.

The assistant scowled at him saying, "This is very irregular."

Nemroz replied, "If you are unsatisfied with me you had better speak to the priest elders."

Darius gave him a terrified look. But he held out his hand to him, and they walked to the small chamber together.

On the stretcher on the floor lay the mutilated body of the 'fallen priest'. Another of the priests brought in the young 'lover'.

He said sneering, "We no longer expect you to enter his wound. You will be anointed with the blood like a worshiper. Then you will consecrate the 'offering'."

Darius looked questioningly at Nemroz, who was looking nervously at the assistants.

One said sarcastically, "Perhaps you wish your 'helper' to do it."

But he was shocked when Nemroz took the small vessel of blood and handed it to Darius. Who looked terrified.

Nemroz gently whispered, "Just masturbate me and apply the liquid."

Though he was unsure in front of the assistants, he did as he was asked. The assistants looked disgusted. But Nemroz performed his duty, then stood, took Darius by the hand and left.

They returned to the sleeping chamber and cleaned each other up, before they sat down on the couch.

Darius asked if he may speak. "Of course you can. What is wrong?"

More outspoken these days, he said in a trembling voice, "My master, I am worried about what you said to the assistants. What will become of us?"

With tears in his eyes, Nemroz replied, "You were to have stayed in here, I should never have weakened and taken you with me. I have put you in danger. Please forgive me."

"I am not worried about what they will do to me. But if they end your ministry…" and his voice faded away.

After a few moments Nemroz replied. "We will face that if it happens."

"But I have learnt to love you. I could not live without you." Then in a whisper he added, "Perhaps they will take me instead."

"Sh, Forgive me. Just hold me." Nemroz felt he was losing control of the situation. He no longer knew what his assistants were doing.

The next morning a call came for Nemroz to attend a new 'offering'. As he went to respond, he insisted that Darius was at least taken some fresh water. The assistant reluctantly obeyed.

Nemroz started the process of teaching his new charge the meaning of the chalices that had been brought. He sat for a while with her calming her fears. But he was pleased to return to Darius.

After the evening ritual meal he insured that two meals were brought to the sleeping chamber. And it was a relief to fill their stomachs.

Life continued with the usual ritual for a while and before any more was heard about the priest's complaint the whole of the temple was wrecked.

Life in the temple was very isolated and the priests led very sheltered lives. They had no idea at first of the uproar that was happening in the city. But it broke threw to their calm ritualistic world.

An army of soldiers broke in, some smashed up the temple, even the great Farago statue itself. Killing all the priests they found. Many scattered and escaped.

Though the assistants had been disgusted with the way Nemroz had behaved, their loyalty still held in a crisis. They smuggled out both Nemroz and Darius.

They got separated from the other priests, but they managed to stay together. Nemroz was very conspicuous in his wonderful cloak and Darius had not managed to have any clothes at all. They were very lucky a worshiper rescued them and took them in and hid them in their home. He found clothes for them, provided food for them and kept them hidden.

The lady of the house often sat with them. She was very interested in who they were. At first they were nervous about saying much. And though Darius never said anything, gradually Nemroz started opening up a bit. And she began to tell him about the invaders who had wrecked the temple.

She told them that they also had priests who travelled with them. But the god they served seemed very different to the god Nemroz served. He seemed to be a god who loved them and did not require the sacrifices that Farago did. Gradually Nemroz became very interested in this god she spoke of, and wanted to know how she knew so much about him. He was told she had been speaking to one of their priests and he seemed keen to inform her all about his god.

Then one day the master of the house came home very agitated, saying, "The soldiers were searching every house looking for priests and worshippers of Farago, or any of the other gods."

He said Nemroz and Darius must leave straight away.

The lady said, "Go to the tent at the far side of the soldiers' camp, where the priests worship. Though they are foreigners they wish us no harm. They may protect you. But keep away from the soldiers.

The family smuggled the both of them out of the city, but they said it was now up to them.

It had been good to have normal meals supplied by their protectors, and not having the responsibilities of Nemroz's duties. But now they, for the first time, had to learn to fend for themselves.

They kept well away from the army camp and headed towards the countryside. By the evening they were well clear of the city and the camp. They found somewhere to hide and tried to sleep.

When the sun dawned next morning, Nemroz through his arms round Darius admitting he had no idea where to find food.

Darius burst into tears when he realized he could not help. "What shall we do?" he sobbed.

Nemroz replied, "The kind lady of the house said the foreign priest would help. Do you think we should risk it?"

"Well we have to do something. We can only die once. We either starve or we risk being killed."

"You are right, we will have to risk it."

They emerged from their hiding place and skirted round the outside of the army camp. They saw a large tent a bit apart from the others. They found somewhere to hide and watched to see if they could get an idea of what was going on.

They saw someone coming and going, who wore robes not unlike they used to wear, only they were black instead of white. They decided to risk it and went to investigate. They crept in. The robed man swung round. They soon found they knew nothing of his language and he knew little of theirs. But they managed to communicate that they were from the city and that they needed help.

The priest did invite them in and shared his own food with them. Nemroz was curious about this deity who loved his worshippers and did not expect the kind of sacrifices that Farago did. But discussing things was hard.

Nemroz and Darius remained with the priest for several days. Nemroz was doing his best to help him to learn their language. Then one dreadful day some soldiers burst into the tent, and arrested Nemroz and Darius. The priest protested, but he was brushed aside. The pair were dragged from the tent, bound and marched to a compound where there were several other prisoners. They were herded like animals and driven with whips back to the city, and to the city's main square. Then to the main administration building. But during that process, Nemroz and Darius got separated.

The next day the priest arrived. He did eventually manage to get some of the prisoners released into his care, including Nemroz. But they were all confined to the rooms in the administration building that were assigned to the priest.

He came to see Nemroz, hoping he would be his best chance to learn the local language, and help to teach the locals about his deity,

Nemroz was pleased to see him, but all he could think about was Darius.

He pleaded with the priest, "If you can return my friend. I will help you as you have asked."

The priest promised to try and left. He arranged for food to be brought to Nemroz and the other prisoners. But he did not return for days.

Poor Nemroz hardly ate or slept. Then at last one day the priest entered the room where the prisoners were held carrying Darius's battered, bleeding body. A distraught Nemroz rushed up to him anxiously asking if he was still alive.

"Just about." The priest replied.

Nemroz gasped, "Can I treat him? Is there somewhere you can lay him?"

The priest was about to just lay him on the floor. Nemroz demanded he needed at least a mattress and somewhere private. The priest looked shocked.

Nemroz continued, "If you expect my help, that is the least I expect in return. But first I need water and something to dress the wounds."

Nemroz fell on his knees by his friend sobbing, "What have they done to you?"

The priest returned saying, "Come with me."

Nemroz gently lifted Darius in his arms and followed the priest into the small room that he used as a sanctuary. The priest brought a bowl of water and some cloth.

"Here, you can use this to clean him and dress the wounds, I will try to get a mattress, but I cannot promise."

Darius was hardly conscious. Nemroz tore the cloth into strips, cleaning the wounds and using other strips to bind them. Then he lay him on his own body to give him a little comfort and keep him off the cold floor. Nemroz hardly ever left him night or day.

The priest brought what supplies he could. Gradually Nemroz helped Darius to take water, and in time he was becoming more conscious, and began to take a little light food. They were only conscious of each other, and not of the chaos going on in the city outside.

Then one day the priest entered with not just the water and broth that he had been bringing for them. He was accompanied by several of his believers, each was carrying other individuals. They all looked very sick. The priest told them to lay them on the floor. Turning to Nemroz he explained, "These are all priests who escaped from the temple, who the believers have rescued from the city. You may know them. I will try to send what help I can, but will you look after them?"

Though Darius was gradually recovering, he still was not strong enough to help look after the others. But he was able to sit with the newcomers to encourage them.

When he first sat with a tall dark haired young man lying in the corner, he cried out with astonishment and relief, "Polto!"

Polto opened his blurry eyes and looked at Darius, who fell down beside him weeping, "My..." (wanting to say, my darling, my love.) He just leaned forward and kissed him. He looked up helplessly at Nemroz, who was tending one of the others.

"Can I have some water for Polto?"

Nemroz stopped and came to his side, "Is it really? Will you be able to manage if I leave the water with you?"

"You know I would always do anything for Polto." He said gazing adoringly at Polto.

Nemroz brought them the water and returned to the young man he was treating. Darius lovingly helped Polto to sip the water.

Darius stayed by Polto's side. When later Nemroz came to see how his old friend Polto was, Darius pleaded, "Can you release me and let me stay with Polto?"

Nemroz responded by saying, "As the temple no longer exists, I am no longer a High Priest, so you are no longer committed to me."

Darius took Nemroz's hand and kissed it, then through his arms around Polto and wept.

Nemroz continued helping the other ex-priests and Darius did not move from Polto's side. He did not seem to have many physical wounds, but he was still very sick. He managed to take any water Darius gave him. But any food, he vomited up.

Darius persisted with tiny amounts of very dilute broth. And gradually the situation improved. With Darius's dedication Polto gradually got better. Until eventually he was eating almost normally. He had to be careful what he ate for the rest of his life. But he definitely owed his life to Darius.

There were by then a lot of ex-priests in the small room and it was getting crowded. Nemroz asked the foreign priest if there was any chance that, Polto, Darius and himself could have a room to themselves. By then a whole portion of the building had been allocated to the priest's use, so he granted the request.

The three of them were well by then. The group was now well established and they were given a couch, as long as they were prepared to share, which pleased Polto and Darius very much. Especially Darius.

What the priest asked in return was that Nemroz helped with translating the texts relating to the new god, into their local language. (Nemroz was the only one among them who could write.)

Each morning Nemroz was taken to the priest's chamber. Where they discussed the texts and worked out a list of the translated words.

After a while Nemroz asked if he might teach Polto and Darius to write. That way they could have two copiers and a translator. The priest agreed. At first they all worked in the priest's chamber, then as the priest began to trust them, a table and chairs were supplied for them in their sleeping chamber, which freed the priest for other duties.

Nemroz spent some of his time teaching Polto and Darius to write. Then while he did the translating the other two were allowed to have some free time together. Darius now had what he had always wanted. As Polto now realized Nemroz was not interested, he was glad to respond to Darius, and Darius was ecstatic.

As Nemroz worked on the texts the priest gave him, he put aside any words he still did not know. He had a time each day to work with the priest on those words, to work out a satisfactory translation. As Nemroz worked on more of these texts, he became more interested in the doctrine.

One day when seeing the priest, he asked to speak to him about becoming a believer. It was arranged that he should meet with a group of other believers.

Nemroz then spoke to Polto and Darius about joining him. Their approach was much more cautious. Though Darius was prepared to come to the meeting. But unfortunately, it came up about the relationship between Darius and Polto.

The believers told Darius that there was something wrong with him and what he did with Polto was disgusting. Poor Darius was very upset and confused.

When they got back to their chamber, he burst into tears, sobbing to Nemroz, "I don't understand what is wrong. I love Polto, I always have."

Nemroz tried to comfort him, "Nor do I understand. I will ask the priest to explain."

A distraught Darius sobbed, "Please do not see the priest anymore."

"I cannot do that. The only reason we were given this room was because I agreed to do the work on the translations with the priest. If I refuse, we will be thrown out."

Darius just looked sad and the subject was dropped for the time being.

But a few days later, a group of believers burst into the chamber, they attacked Darius and Polto, and also verbally abused them. Nemroz was furious and did eventually manage to throw them out. He was scared to leave them alone after that. When the attendant came to fetch him, he just thrust the papers at him saying, "This is all I have managed to do today."

The next day when the next batch of papers was brought he stood at the doorway saying, "I cannot do any today, I am not well."

The attendant left. But later in the day the priest came to see what was the matter. Nemroz could hardly refuse him entrance. Nemroz motioned to the other two to leave it to him.

He asked the priest to take a seat. He started by questioning him about what was said at the meeting with the believers. The priest explained that intimacy should only be between a man and a woman and then only between a married couple.

Nemroz responded with, "What if a man deeply loves a man?"

"That is wrong."

Darius was cringing and burying his head in Polto's lap.

Nemroz continued, "Is it right that a whole gang of believers should attack a man just for being in love?"

Violence is never justified.

"Well a group of your followers burst in here, beat Polto and Darius and shouted at them, when all they were doing was working on your texts."

The priest looked shocked and said he would look into the matter. Nemroz rose indicating the priest should leave. The priest looked surprised, but did not resist.

As soon as he left Darius ran to Nemroz and fell at his feet. Polto came more calmly to sit at the table and on the way saying under his breath, "I knew I was right getting you appointed as leader."

Then all three of them just sat in silence.

For the next few days nothing happened. Not even texts arrived. They did not know what to do. They went to collect their food, but instead of eating with the others as usual they brought it back to their chamber.

Then one fateful day, Polto and Darius were on the couch together when several vengeful believers burst into the chamber. One grabbed Darius and threw him against the wall, and two more grabbed Polto and threw him against the wall at the other end of the chamber.

At first all three were too stunned to move. Then Nemroz ran to lift Darius and laid him on the couch. Polto rose himself and came unsteadily to join them.

Darius looked dazed as he said, "What happened?"

Nemroz collected himself and replied bitterly, "The priest cannot keep control of his followers."

Polto was trembling with fury, "We are leaving here!" he growled.

"But where will we go?" Darius pleaded.

It was Polto who took charge of the situation this time. After the evening meal he stated, he was leaving and he was taking Darius with him.

He turned to Nemroz and asked, "Are you coming with us?"

"If they treat you like that, there is no way I will let you leave without me."

The three of them sneaked out as soon as it was dark. Nemroz was amazed Polto knew his way around so well. But he would not explain how. They got out of the building and found their way through the dark streets. By the time they reached the outskirts of the city it was getting light. Polto said, they must find somewhere to hide.

They did not sleep much, but eventually it went dark again. They continued like that for several nights. Sometimes they found streams where they could drink, but none of them knew where to find food.

Polto was worried about that. But Darius said, "We have lived without food before."

Nemroz looked at him sadly saying, "I am sorry about that."

Then one morning as it was getting light, Polto whispered, "Look, that looks like a farm down there."

The others looked a little blank.

"If it is, that means there are people and possibly food. It is not likely to be the invaders, if it is a farm."

"Should we go and see?" said Darius enthusiastically.

It was decided they would risk it, and they made their way down to the farm, footsore, weary and very hungry. As they approached there seemed to be no one about. They tried the outbuildings, all seemed deserted. So they approached the cottage. They cautiously entered the kitchen. At first they thought the cottage was deserted as well, when they heard a movement.

Polto called, "We are not here to harm anyone, we need help."

A very scared young girl crawled out of her hiding place.

Polto announced, "We have escaped from the city, and we haven't eaten for days."

The girl just stood there looking scared at first.

Then Polto continued, "Are you here alone?"

She stuttered, "My mistress is hiding."

"Can you fetch her?"

"My mistress will not be pleased."

"Please! We need help." Nemroz pleaded.

Still rather unsure, she disappeared, returning soon with another girl.

Polto tried again, "Are you here alone?"

The girl replied, "We were raided by the army. The only men left were killed or taken with them. All our supplies and animals were taken. I think there may be some maids left, but they are hiding."

"Do you have any food left at all?"

"There are a few vegetables that are still in the field." She paused then said, "My sister has gone to find help."

"Do you at least have something to drink?" Darius asked plaintively.

The girl suddenly pulled herself together. "Yes of course. Please sit down." She turned to the maid and told her to draw some water. When she returned, her mistress filled three beakers and passed them to the bedraggled visitors.

"I am so sorry I have nothing else to offer you."

They sat talking for a while. Polto decided it was safe to tell their host who they were. And she told them what had happened to the family and the farm. Also that her name was Arlaya. She asked if they would help her. The three of them summoned what little strength they had left and followed her to the field.

They helped gather the remaining vegetables, not returning to the cottage until the afternoon. They collapsed onto the kitchen chairs. Soon after that Arlaya's sister returned. She had brought some food, some of which the maid started to prepare.

She also had good news, she had made it to their uncle's farm. He was prepared to take them in and share what little they had.

Later when Arlaya and her sister Garetta were alone, Arlaya explained who the three strange gentlemen were, and they discussed whether they should offer to take them with them to their uncle's. They decided as there were so few males around any more, that had not been killed or taken by the army, that their uncle would probably be glad of their help. But what should they do with them tonight.

When they returned to the kitchen all three of them were asleep across the table, so they left them there.

Next day the sisters still could not find any more of the maids, so they reluctantly decided to leave just the six of them.

There was little they could take, but Garetta did feel safer having three men with them. They had to walk all day to reach the farm, which was hard after what the three of them had been through. But at least they had now had some food. They arrived at the outer limit of the farm by evening.

Arlaya asked the three of them to wait there while the others continued down to see her uncle. He was an elderly man, too old now to do work on the farm. He had lost most of his family. Arlaya and Garetta went and told him about their companions. At first he was not sure, but he did agree that even a few men on the farm would help.

It was Garetta who said, "We can't just leave them up there. Can I ask them to join us?"

Reluctantly because they had little food for themselves, eventually he agreed. The maid stayed and joined in with preparing the meal, while Arlaya and Garetta went back to fetch the others. They all ate together with the farm staff (who were all maids) in the kitchen.

After the meal the family discussed who could sleep where. The uncle (who everyone just called Pops), said the girls could sleep with his daughter Terrace, the maid could sleep in the servants' quarters "But what can we do with your friends?"

Nemroz suggested they slept in the barn.

"That's not right." Arlaya protested.

Polto agreed that would be fine. Darius was happy, as long as he could lie with Polto.

Nemroz asked if it was acceptable for them to retire straight away as they were all exhausted.

They found a comfortable spot in the hayloft, and prepared for sleep. Darius looked longingly at Polto. But Polto insisted he was exhausted, but he said, "I will lie with you tomorrow."

Darius just looked sad, but he did not argue. He just went to sleep. Nemroz lay beside them as well.

The next morning the three of them crossed the yard and nervously entered the kitchen in the cottage. A few of the maids were already preparing the breakfasts. They were relieved when they were greeted with a friendly "Good morning."

When they hesitated one of the maids said, "Take a seat, the family will be in soon."

It was Arlaya who came in first. She said, "Good morning. Was it all right in the barn? Did you sleep okay?"

They all replied in unison, "Yes, it was good thanks."

It was Nemroz who asked, "What will we be expected to do today?"

She replied, "You will have to ask Pops, he will be here in a while."

By the time breakfast was served all had arrived except Pops. But he arrived soon after. Once breakfast was cleared away, it was Polto this time who asked Pops what they should do each day.

At first Pops said, "This is rather a strange situation. It will be helpful to have some males around, but from what the girls say you know nothing about farm life."

"I am afraid not sir."

"At first you can carry and lift things for the girls. But I will need to teach you how the farm works. I am too old to do much myself, so I hope you can just be told what to do."

"We will do our best sir."

"Less of the sir, just call me Pops." He continued. Addressing Nemroz he said, "Arlaya is taking over the milking, so if you go with her, you can help with lifting the milk pail etc. As for you two, come with me and I will try to teach you the work in the fields."

Polto and Darius left with Pops. And Nemroz stayed with Arlaya. They went and fetched the cow, and brought her to the milking shed. Nemroz watched with interest as Arlaya fetched the stool and the pail and proceeded with the milking. Nemroz tried to make conversation, but Arlaya was very shy when she was on her own with Nemroz.

Then he said, ""Please do not be afraid of me. I would not harm you. What do you know of the Farago priests?"

She hesitated before she answered, "Only that they kill young girls."

Nemroz cringed, "And what do you know of the High Priest?"

"Much the same I would imagine."

"That is where you are wrong."

"Oh yes, and what do you know about it."

"I know because I am he."

"You expect me to believe that?"

"What can I do to prove it?"

She went quiet and continued with the milking.

When she finished she turned to Nemroz and said, "Are you going to lift the pail for me?"

"Of course, where should I take it?"

"Well first lift it away from the cow, so that she will not kick it over."

Arlaya returned the stool to where she got it from. And released the cow's halter. She led the cow, and Nemroz carried the pail.

As they crossed the yard Arlaya said, "You take the milk to the kitchen."

Nemroz put the pail on the kitchen floor, not sure what to do next. He was still there feeling rather useless when Arlaya returned. "You still here?" Arlaya said.

"I was not sure what else needed doing." Nemroz replied.

Arlaya showed Nemroz where to put the milk, then said, "Come and sit with me for a while."

Nemroz was surprised as she had been so reluctant to talk to him in the milking shed. Still sounding a little shy, she said, "Please tell me more about this temple of yours."

Nemroz was shocked and did not know where to begin.

Arlaya prompted, "How did you come to be at the temple?"

He could cope with that. He told how he was donated as a baby. Then how he became leader of the rebels. But when it came to him as High Priest he collapsed. He was nearly in tears. His voice faded away and he stopped.

"What is wrong?" Arlaya said with concern.

"Maybe one day I will be able to tell you." He whispered. After a few minutes he rushed from the room. He staggered across the yard and stood with his head against the barn door. When there was no one in the yard to ease his pain. He stumbled up to the hayloft, and lay there weeping the rest of the day.

Later the other two came in the barn to put their tools away, chattering excitedly about the farm and what they had been doing. Not knowing that Nemroz was close by in the hayloft. While they were all in the city Nemroz had never been jealous of the other two and their closeness. Even when he sat on the floor while they lay together. But now their chatter hurt. Polto and Darius left and returned to the kitchen in the cottage.

Nemroz could not face the others. He no longer felt hungry, he felt sick.

Everyone else collected in the kitchen for their meal. At first no one even noticed that Nemroz was not there. It was Darius who asked, "Where is Nemroz?"

Arlaya replied, "He went out earlier."

But no one went looking for him.

Polto and Darius were concerned. They walked to the field, thinking Nemroz had come looking for them. But when they could not find him they just said, "He will turn up." And returned to the barn. Not realizing he was in the barn all the time. They climbed to the hayloft and lay together, not thinking to look for Nemroz in the hayloft.

It was not until next morning Darius realized he had not found Nemroz, and cried out, "We did not find Nemroz!" He heard a sob and began to frantically search for him. He found him half covered with hay, down against the side wall of the hayloft.

He cried, "I have found him." Then to Nemroz he said, "Why didn't you join us?"

"You had each other, no one wanted me."

"We had always wanted you, even if you do not have a desire for us the way we have for each other."

They through their arms round each other, and for the moment it eased Nemroz's pain. The three of them crossed to the farm kitchen for breakfast.

By the time they got there, most of the family were already there.

Arlaya looked up looking concerned. "Did I upset you yesterday?"

"It was not your fault. You were not to know that the memories of the temple are still very painful. Please think no more of it." Nemroz replied.

Before anyone could say anything else Darius said, "It is all right we will look after him." Nemroz gave Darius a grateful smile.

After breakfast all three of them went to see Pops about what they should do.

He asked, "Shall I send someone else to help with the milk pail?"

Nemroz quickly replied, "No I would love to help, but I would appreciate having other things to help with the rest of the day."

"Fine, I will get one of the maids to bring you to the field."

Arlaya cut in, "I will bring him Pops."

Pops, Polto and Darius left for the field as they had done before. Arlaya and Nemroz left to fetch the cow.

Nemroz gazed at her and said, "There is so much I need to know, please help me."

"Be patient with me, I am not used to men."

"Please believe me I would never harm you."

"Perhaps, but you are very different to any other man. I cannot understand how I hurt you."

"Please forgive me. I will keep my feelings under control." Nothing more was said.

Neither of them dared say anything while Arlaya was doing the milking. But Nemroz was aware of feelings for Arlaya. He was worried and confused. Would that be acceptable now. As they walked back across the yard Arlaya said, "You know now where the milk needs to go. Meet me back in the yard."

He was horrified when he heard himself say, "Yes my dear one." And he hurried into the kitchen. He poured the milk into the cooler. He was in the yard first. He paused wondering whether he was right to wait or run. He decided to walk towards the field where the cow grazed. Arlaya greeted him with a smile and showed him the way to where Polto and Darius were working. Then she returned to the cottage.

His friends were pleased that he had joined them, and it was easier for Nemroz having something to keep him occupied. He went first to Pops, and he instructed him what he should do. The three of them spent the day sowing, planting and tending the vegetables.

It was a long tiring day. But it was more satisfying working out in the field. They returned to the cottage for the meal in the evening. Nemroz managed to sit by Arlaya at the table.

She whispered to him, "Before you go to the barn. Can I see you?"

"Of course."

"Wait for me in the yard."

When the meal was finished the three of them left.

As soon as they were outside Nemroz said, "You two go on, I will join you later."

Darius replied, "Are you alright?"

"Yes, I am fine. I want to talk to Arlaya."

They left, and Nemroz waited nervously.

Soon Arlaya joined him saying, "Shall we sit in the milking shed?"

Nothing more was said until they were sat together on a pile of straw in the cow shed.

Nemroz was gazing at Arlaya when she said. "Are you alright?"

"Yes, I am fine. I was just wondering whether it is right for me to respond to you."

Arlaya looked frightened, so Nemroz quickly added, "I would never do anything you do not want me to, but I should not respond to a woman."

"You are very strange."

"One day I will explain." Then under his breath he added, "But please do not ask me now."

Arlaya decided to risk putting her arms round him. He felt her nervousness, so he said, "Please can you tell me about your family, or is that difficult for you."

"You are very kind. Would it be safe to kiss you?"

Nemroz looked shocked. "No one has ever asked me that before."

Arlaya looked surprised, "Have you never been with a woman before?"

"My experience of women is very different. I would not expect you to understand. One day I will cope with telling you."

"You are very strange."

"It is sad we have both had so much hurt. Maybe we should just leave the past alone, for the time being."

Without asking again she threw her arms round him and kissed him. He was amazed. For quite a while Nemroz just sat there enjoying the experience without the threat of the 'punishment' hanging over him.

Then at last Arlaya said. "I really must get back."

Before Nemroz let her go he asked, "Can I see you again?"

"You will see me in the morning."

Nemroz looked disappointed, but he left it at that. Arlaya returned to the cottage and Nemroz went to the barn.

He stood at the bottom of the ladder and called, "Is it okay to come up?"

Darius replied, "Fine, come and join us."

Polto was more subdued he said, "Where have you been?"

At first Nemroz was not sure whether to say, but he decided as now Polto seemed happy with Darius he said, "I went to see Arlaya."

"What for?"

Darius butted in, "REALLY Polto!" And all went quiet.

Next morning when they went for breakfast Arlaya was already there. She greeted Nemroz with, "Please sit here by me."

Darius made sure Polto left that seat for Nemroz, whispering in Polto's ear, "What is the matter with you?"

Polto snarled and sat on the next seat along and Nemroz gave him a hurt look. After breakfast the three of them reported to Pops.

"Right we have done all we need with the vegetables for now. I will try to teach you as much as I can about the rest of the farm. But I can't give you a tour of the farm, my legs aren't up to it. First you had better go with Arlaya, Nemroz, but come back as soon as you can."

"Thankyou sir." Nemroz said, hurrying out, looking to Arlaya as he went. She followed.

As they walked to the meadow Arlaya said, "Perhaps I should teach you to milk the cow, as the pail is too heavy for me to carry."

Nemroz looked at her sadly, "Do you not want to be with me now. Have I hurt you?"

"No, of course you haven't."

"Then please let me be with you."

She grinned at him and said, "You are sweet."

Nemroz was not sure how to take that remark, and walked on in silence.

While Arlaya was doing the milking, he gazed at her and said. "I so want you to talk to me."

She replied, "Will you come again tonight?"

"I would love to."

"If I talk to you. Will you tell me about the temple?"

"Oh my darling… I will try." He did not say another word. As they crossed the yard, Arlaya said. "There is no need to come to the meadow, you are to go straight to the kitchen, to join the other two."

"I wish you could teach me about the farm."

"It's not the farm I know, you go to Pops. I will see you later."

Pops spent the day explaining all that they had before the invaders took a lot of what they had and most of his family. Maybe in time we will have a herd of cows and a flock of sheep again. Will it be in time for me to be here to teach you how to care for them? There are the vegetables that I have been teaching you about, but there were fields of wheat but now there is no one to till the fields and no oxen or horses to pull a plough. The three ex-priests just sat there looking confused.

"How can we learn about all that, I feel so helpless." Pops did his best to explain how to keep cows and sheep and plough the fields, but they did not really understand.

Later the maids came to start on the meal, but there was only vegetables and cheese. Later Garetta and her cousin Terrace joined

37

them. Pops asked them how much they know about the keeping of sheep and cows.

"Not much, the boys mostly did that." Terrace said, "If Arlaya's friends can come with us tomorrow, we will show them what we know."

By the time the meal was ready Arlaya had joined them as well. Polto glared at the chairs and sat on the fifth seat along. When the meal was over, Polto and Darius went to the barn, and Arlaya and Nemroz went to the cow shed.

As soon as they were inside and the door was closed, Arlaya through her arms round Nemroz saying, "Is this alright?"

"Yes you are wonderful."

"Are you going to be upset tonight?"

"I will try not to. What do you want to know?"

Arlaya gazed nervously at him. "When you were High Priest, what did you do?" When he did not answer, she continued, "Did you kill young girls?"

"Not myself no."

"Did you know the girls that…"

Nemroz looked away and softly said, "Yes my dear, I did."

"How could you?"

Nemroz was fighting back his emotions, he had not expected an onslaught like this. Eventually he said as calmly as he could, "I had to."

"What did YOU do?" she repeated.

"I shared the ritual meals with them, and explained what they meant."

Then before she said anymore he cried, "No more please!"

She stopped and through her arms round him again saying, I am sorry I did not mean to hurt you. He could not manage any questions in return and just said, "We should go now."

"Can we meet again tomorrow night?"

"If you want to."

"I will try not to hurt you, I promise."

"Can I kiss you good-night?"

"Oh yes."

"Do you still trust me after what I have told you?"

"I am sure it was not your fault. I will see you tomorrow."

He kissed her again and left. He crept quietly to the back of the hayloft and slid in beside the other two.

It was not until they woke next morning that Darius asked Nemroz, "Were you alright last night?"

Before he had chance to answer, Polto cut in, "He was fine, he was with Arlaya."

Darius retorted, Polto, what is the matter with you?"

Polto just snorted.

After freshening themselves at the trough by the well, they went to breakfast.

CHAPTER

After breakfast, Garetta and Terrace took the three to see as much as they could in connection to cow rearing and sheep rearing. At that time there was only one cow and a few sheep. They had no one capable of killing and butchering either.

All three of them together said, "I wish there was more we could do."

After the evening meal Nemroz and Arlaya went to the cow shed.

"Pops is getting worried about us being alone together."

"What can I do to persuade him you are safe?"

"Pops says Terrace must come too."

"But I need you on your own. I would never do you any harm. Can I be frank?"

"Yes."

"I would never enter you, even if you asked me."

Arlaya looked quite shocked. She realized that remark was also something to do with the temple, so she said. "What did you do with the ladies in the temple?"

He hugged her and said, "Please don't."

"I will find a way. We need to get to know about each other."

"Would you believe you are safe to lie with me?"

"I think so."

"I could not do that with Terrace here."

"That is why Pops wants her here."

They gently lay in each other's arms. Though Arlaya was very nervous at first. But Nemroz was as reliable as he had said.

"Are you sure you are not like your friends?"

"I am a normal man. I have just learnt great control."

Then Nemroz said, "I should go now."

He saw Arlaya safely to the cottage as by then it was dark. He returned to the barn, and went straight up to the hayloft. He was glad to find Polto was against the wall.

He whispered to Darius, "Are you awake?"

"Is that you Nemroz?"

"Yes, can I ask you something?"

"What do you want?"

"I am out of practise with that level of control. Can I lie with you?"

"It is a long time since you have asked for that. Yes of course you can." He giggled, "You will need to look like a High Priest again."

Nemroz undressed and lay with Darius. But Polto was annoyed when he woke next morning and found him like that.

Before they set out for breakfast Darius asked to know more about what was going on. At first Nemroz seemed reluctant.

Darius reminded him, "Surely we were close enough for you to trust me, for you to tell me."

"I was with Arlaya last night. I am beginning to want her, but I have promised not to touch her."

"If ever you need me I am still here."

Polto was dressing, but he butted in, "Darius is not here for your disposal now that you are no longer a High Priest."

But Darius came back with, "Take no notice of him. I don't know what is the matter with him these days."

Polto just turned and went. After breakfast Nemroz and Arlaya left to fetch the cow.

"Nemroz I trust you. But Pops doesn't."

"Can you go to the cow shed tonight?"

"I will come if I can."

Nemroz looked very sad. He felt ashamed when he said, "You will be with your sister. Polto and Darius will be together. I don't want to be alone."

"If I am too long coming go to your friends."

Nemroz gave her a quick kiss. Then admitted, "I love you."

After the meal that night Nemroz did go to the cow shed. He felt sad and alone. But he was trying to believe that Arlaya would come if she could. He was about to leave when he heard the rattle of the latch. He jumped up and when he heard Arlaya's soft voice through the near darkness, he rushed to her side. He swept her into his arms and carried her to the pile of straw.

"I had to wait until Pops went to bed." She whispered.

"I don't want to get you into trouble, but it is wonderful to be with you."

"I want to find a way for us to be together."

"I know we have not been together for long, but would you be prepared to be my wife?"

Arlaya gasped, "Please let me think about it."

"Of course, can I lie beside you?"

"Do I dare stay here with you?" she muttered almost to herself. "No one would know where we are."

"I would love it very much. But I do not want the others worrying about where I am"

"I do love you. I will try to come tomorrow. Tell your friends you might stay here. I will see what Garetta and Terrace think. I must go now. I am so sorry."

Nemroz gave her a big kiss and they left.

Arlaya still sat by Nemroz at mealtimes, but she had nothing to say for herself, not even to her sister on the other side of her. After the evening meal once the three were in the yard, Nemroz explained he may not be in the barn that night. Polto just grunted, but Darius said, "Be careful."

Nemroz went to the cow shed, worried he would be alone. He had not been alone since the early days of being High Priest, and they were not happy memories.

He was sure that Arlaya was not coming, and he tried unsuccessfully to sleep. At last he heard the rattle of the latch and he cried. "Arlaya is that you?"

She did not answer, but she rushed to his side sobbing. He through his arms round her saying, "What is the matter my darling?"

"I have been arguing with the family. They say I should not marry a stranger. I know your world was very different to ours, but you are not a foreigner and I love you so much."

"Oh, my dear, if I had somewhere safe to take you I would run away with you."

"If I lay with you they would have no choice."

"That would be wrong."

"Could you not do that for me?"

Nemroz hesitated, "I have never really done that with any woman." Then with a shudder he added, "If I did, I would have been put to death."

Arlaya sobbed and said, "One day you will tell me about that dreadful place. But that is behind you now."

"Deep-down I am still a High Priest. I do not know that I should take a wife at all."

"The temple is no more. And I want you so much."

"Please." He begged. "This is tearing me apart."

"If even you are not on my side, I do not want to live."

"Oh, my dear Arlaya, I would love you to be my wife."

"Then forget the dreadful temple and take me!"

Nemroz just broke down and sobbed.

Eventually Arlaya was sobbing too. "Help me, your pain is more than I can take."

"Any man's control has its limits." He howled.

"Far be it for me to test you beyond your limits. But surely if you want me and I want you…" her voice faded away.

"At lease I will die happy." And he almost gave in. Then he just grabbed her and pressed himself against her.

"Press yourself against me as hard as you can. I am sorry that is the best I can manage as things are."

As the sun rose next morning Arlaya gazed at him and said, "Nemroz you are amazing."

He just sobbed and replied, "I am sorry."

She was suddenly scared of what was happening. She jumped up saying, "I can't face the family at breakfast."

Nemroz felt like saying 'You should have thought of that last night,' but he didn't. He did say, "I will take the blame."

"But it was not your fault, and you didn't do anything wrong."

"No, I didn't do anything."

"No, I must face them. I can't let you take the blame." Then she insisted, "We must face them together."

They waited until the others had all gone for breakfast. Then they walked across together. They nervously entered the kitchen. All eyes were on them as Pops asked crossly, "Where do you think you have been?"

After a long pause Arlaya announced, "I need to be married."

Pops flew into a rage, "Why, what has he done to you?"

"Nemroz was the perfect gentleman. But you nor anyone else should make him wait for ever. We love each other."

"I only have your word for that. Does he not have a tongue of his own?"

Nemroz gave Arlaya's hand a little squeeze before he began, "I am very grateful for all that you have done for all three of us. But Arlaya and I love each other. I wish sir for your permission to marry your niece."

There was a silence, and all eyes were on Pops.

"You are not suitable to marry my niece."

Arlaya pleaded, "If anything it is me who is not worthy of him. He would not agree to any impure suggestion. Though the city temple was smashed down, he is still a High Priest at heart."

"You want to marry a High Priest?" Pops sneered.

"That would be a great honour, besides I love him very much. You say he is not suitable. Who in our family could claim to be married to a priest, let alone a High Priest?"

"Get out. Let your priest provide for you."

Arlaya ran from the room, and a distraught Nemroz ran after her. When he caught up with her, he swung her into his arms sobbing, "Your uncle is right, I am not suitable. I cannot provide for you."

"I would rather starve than turn down your proposal."

"Come sit in the cow shed. We will think this through."

They were still there when Garetta came with the cow. She turned away.

"Please do not mind us. Nemroz is not doing anything he shouldn't."

"My dear sister, I am sure Pops will come round."

Nemroz sadly replied, "But I cannot provide for her. What use is a priest."

Arlaya ran to fetch the pail and the stool for her sister. Garetta turned to her and asked, "Do you really love him and want him what ever the cost?"

"I would die for him."

"We are not asking for that. And you Nemroz, are you honourable and do you truly love my sister?"

"With all my heart."

"Then we will have to find a way to look after you both. Would you be prepared to stay in the cow shed?"

"Anywhere, but I need him now!"

"You say you are priests. Would your friends be able to declare you married?"

"We are not that kind of priests."

They were both surprise when she said, "The family will not know that. If you can persuade your friends to do that, I am sure Terrace and some of the maids will attend."

"Garetta you are wonderful. I will finish the milking."

As Garetta was about to leave Nemroz asked, "Could you ask Polto and Darius to come here?"

She agreed and left. As soon as they were alone again Nemroz said, "Am I really to have a wife? Is it really right that I should have a wife?"

"Do you really love me and want me?"

"More than anything else in the world."

"Then forget about the temple, and enjoy it."

"If only it was that easy."

In exasperation Arlaya just kissed him. When she finished the milking Nemroz took the pail and Arlaya put the stool away.

"You take the cow back and I will take the milk."

"Do be careful." Arlaya said. In a worried tone.

"I will be fine. I will see you back in the shed."

But crossing the yard, Darius was walking towards them, "Give that to me. You better keep out of sight for now."

Nemroz replied, "Take the milk to Garetta or one of the maids. Then find Polto and join us in the shed."

Nemroz returned to the shed, and was soon joined by Darius, Arlaya and Garetta. Nemroz asked Darius where Polto was.

"He is not happy about all this."

"Will he join us?"

"I am not sure. I am worried about Polto, he is not usually like this."

Nemroz would normally have been worried, but he had his mind on other things.

It was Darius who started things off, wanting to know what was involved with a marriage. Also he did not think he was worthy. After all he was never more than a trainee priest. But Polto was not interested. Arlaya and Garetta tried to explain what weddings were like in their part of the world. Adding Nemroz would explain what marriage is like afterwards. Slightly confused he listened as he was told what he would need to do.

After they had discussed what was involved with the wedding Garetta turned to Nemroz.

"You are not to sleep with Arlaya before the wedding. You can be with your friends, but it will be rather difficult for Arlaya. We cannot have her alone in a cow shed. Would it be best if I stay with you tonight? I do not think you should come in the cottage. I will bring your meal, then stay with you if that is alright?"

"I will ask Terrace if she will attend, and perhaps some of the maids." All was settled for the next day.

When it came to the evening meal. Garetta brought one for Arlaya, and Darius brought one for Nemroz. Garetta settled to stay the night, and Nemroz left with Darius.

When they entered the barn, Polto was waiting for them. The two friends were astounded by Polto's reaction, he greeted them with, "You should not be getting married. High Priests, in fact any priest should not take a wife."

Ignoring the fact that he was struggling with that himself he reminded Polto that, "The temple no longer exists, so I am no longer a High Priest."

"Nonsense." shouted Polto.

"Come on let's go up." Said Darius calmly.

"You...You... Are not sleeping with us!" Polto shouted, in more of a rage than ever.

Darius was too scared to intervene, Polto turned and climbed the ladder. Darius and Nemroz stood and looked at each other. After a few stunned moments, Darius put his arms round Nemroz and asked quietly, "Is there anywhere down here where we can sleep tonight?"

"We have slept on the hard floor before." commented Nemroz.

They snuggled in among the old farm equipment.

Darius was crying. Nemroz asked, "What is the matter?"

"I am scared of Polto. I never thought I would be scared of my darling Polto. With you gone I am scared of being alone." Darius was struggling with very different painful memories.

This was tearing Nemroz apart. He thought Darius was secure with Polto. He was aware that Polto still had problems from his time in the city, but he had never managed to get him to talk about it.

They were both awake early next morning. Darius said nervously, "I am worried about Polto."

"Yes, so am I. Polto has never been like this, but I am not sure that reasoning with him is going to help."

"You are alright, you have Arlaya. What am I going to do?"

"If we get through today, just be as normal as you can with him and hope that helps."

"You know I would do anything for him. What happens if he finds out I am helping with the wedding?"

"We will make out we have forced you. It is not your fault. You are there against your will. He already blames me."

"Nemroz I am scared."

"I know you are, but I do not think Polto would harm you."

"I know you said the temple is no more. But to me you are still my master and you mean a lot to me."

"My dear sweet friend, you mean a lot to me as well."

Darius through his arms round Nemroz, his voice cracking with emotion he said, "Do you mean that?"

"We will leave before Polto is awake. I will wait outside. You go and see if anyone is up yet."

Darius soon returned saying, "The maids are up, soon breakfast will be ready. But I don't think you should eat with Pops."

"But I should not go to Arlaya either."

"You hide behind the cow shed, I will bring some breakfast when I can." And they parted.

Several maids knew what was going on, and they gave Darius some breakfast to take to Nemroz before Pops came for breakfast. Darius brought two, to keep out of Polto's way.

As they sat and ate Darius sobbed, "I hate keeping out of Polto's way. What can I do? I still love him."

Nemroz was so sad, he nearly had Arlaya, and Darius was losing Polto.

They heard Polto crossing the yard, ranting and raving about Darius staying with Nemroz, instead of coming to him. But Darius wept, "The one thing I want more than anything else is to be with him. Why can't he realize that?"

After breakfast Terrace brought breakfast for Arlaya and Garetta. She told them Pops seems calmer this morning, but we had to make up stories about where you are. Polto looked very disbelieving, we thought he was going to drop us in it.

It was decided to go ahead as soon as Garetta had finished the milking. But who would carry the pail of milk? Garetta and Terrace carried it between them.

All those attending assembled in the cow shed, and Terrace went to find Nemroz and Darius.

Arlaya and Nemroz declared themselves to each other. And Darius as an independent and pretending he was a priest, declared them man and wife. There was none of the usual sacrifices, gifts and feasting. The couple were just led to the bed on the straw, and everyone left. Darius felt deserted and was terrified.

He slunk back into the cow shed weeping, "I should not be here, this time is for you two to be together. But I am terrified what Polto's reaction will be. Please protect me."

"My dear friend this is so sad, we must get Polto to take you back, none of this is your fault."

"When we were in the city you often waited on the floor while I was with Polto. Please just let me hide, I will not watch."

"My dear friend, that is not fair on Arlaya. I do so wish there was someone for you to be with. We must be bold and approach Polto."

"If you go to Polto he will not see you, and there is no knowing what he will do."

"You must go to him, I will stay at a distance to check you are safe, but I do not think he will hurt you."

"Oh, Nemroz that is the one thing I want, but I am so scared."

"Do forgive me for leaving you at this time of all times, but poor Darius has no one else to help him."

"You must do this, I feel it is us that have brought this on your friend, I will wait for you."

Together they looked for Polto but Nemroz kept at a distance. They found him in the barn weeping.

Darius went gently up to him and put his arms round him. "Please do not weep I am still here for you."

Darius was trying hard not to sound scared, but he was terrified. At first Polto did not move. Then slowly he turned to Darius saying, "Will you still come to the gallery with me?"

"Oh my dear Polto, that is what I want more than anything else in the world."

They climbed the ladder in silence. Nemroz felt so torn. He wanted to stay to be sure that Darius was safe. But he wanted to be with Arlaya even more.

Nemroz crept away and returned to Arlaya. She held out her arms to him saying. "Is your friend alright?"

"I think so, I hope things stay that way." He paused then said, "Arlaya I want you."

She caught his hand and drew him down to her. He gazed at her saying, "Am I really allowed to have a wife? Will they not…" and his voice faded away.

"My darling. What did they do to you?"

"I cannot expect you to understand, but you are so patient with me." He lay down beside her saying, "Can we just lie together as we did the other night for now?"

"Will you come to me properly later?"

"I will do my best. But you cannot understand what this is doing to me." Arlaya's patience was fraying. "If you cannot come to me you should not have asked me to marry you."

Nemroz turned away and wept. "Please do not be cross with me. I so want you to help."

He grabbed her and pressed himself to her. Arlaya left it for then and just lay with him until Garetta came with the meal.

"Pops is becoming suspicious. What should we tell him?"

Nemroz ignored the question and asked whether Polto and Darius came for their meal.

"No they didn't." Garetta stated

"I must go and ask if they are alright." Nemroz replied.

"My darling will that be safe?" said Arlaya nervously.

"I do not believe Polto would hurt Darius or me, and it would not be right for the ladies to go."

Both women rushed after him, but he calmly and resolutely walked into the barn. At the bottom of the ladder he called, "Do you two want a meal brought over?"

After a few moments Darius crawled over to the edge of the gallery.

"What has happened to you? Please forgive me I never thought he would hurt you. Are you able to climb down the ladder?"

With Nemroz's help he slid down and he collapsed at his feet. Nemroz picked him up and gently carried him to the cottage. Arlaya was begging him, "No." but he calmly carried him into the kitchen and laid him on the table.

Between them the ladies cleaned and dressed his wounds. Nemroz sat beside him, holding his hand sobbing, "Forgive me, please forgive me."

After some time Darius opened his eyes and in a faint whisper said, "How could he do this? I love him."

Nemroz asked for some milk to be brought, and he helped him to drink it. Then he demanded that there was somewhere comfortable found for him. A stunned Pops was still at the table and he said, "You are mad, all three of you!"

But the ladies rallied round. Terrace said. "Come with me."

Nemroz took Darius in his arms and followed her. They went into a small room where he had never been before. There was a small couch and Nemroz laid Darius on it.

Arlaya had followed them. Nemroz looked helplessly at her saying, "What can I do? I want to be with you."

Darius opened his eyes, and in a weak whisper said, "You should be with Arlaya, please leave me."

Terrace stepped in and said, "I will stay with Darius, you should be with Arlaya, it is your wedding day."

"Please take good care of him. I love both of you. I can't be in two places at once."

"It's alright, I will take good care of him. You stay in the shed for tonight. Then we must sort something better."

"Please forgive me. Please survive." Then to Terrace he said, "Take good care of him. He has meant a lot to me for many years."

Then he took Arlaya by the hand and ran from the room. He ran to the cow shed. Then when they were inside he took her in his arms and sobbed, "It should never have been like this. I want you so much. Please help me. If I die for it, I will die happy."

Arlaya did not know what to say.

Nemroz stripped, then gently removed Arlaya's clothes. He was trembling. He lay her down gently saying again, "Please help me, my body wants you so much, but my mind is screaming."

"My darling, what have they done to you?" he gently entered her sobbing, "Please respond, I can't do this alone."

Between them they worked out what to do, and Nemroz succeeded. And he was gasping, "Priest or not, you really are my wife now."

They went to sleep happy in each other's arms. But in the night Nemroz was screaming in his sleep. Arlaya shook him shouting, "What is the matter?"

He looked at her through bleary eyes. "I must have been dreaming. I was paying the price for what I did with you."

"It is alright, that is all over now."

Next morning they were still in each other's arms when Garetta came with their breakfasts. Nemroz kissed Arlaya as he rose to fetch the clothes, saying. "Please forgive me for waking you."

Arlaya replied, "It is not your fault. I hope in time we will ease your pain."

After they had eaten Nemroz said, "I must go to see Darius."

"Is that wise?"

"I should never have left him. I will not leave him now."

Arlaya collected the plates saying, "I will come with you."

Everyone looked surprised when Nemroz strode in, and went straight to the room where Darius lay. Pops was shouting, "Where do you think you are going?"

But Nemroz ignored him. Darius was still very sore and very weak. But he was more conscious than he had been the night before. Terrace had managed to get him to take some breakfast. He was so pleased to see Nemroz. First he asked, "Was it good last night?"

"It was wonderful!"

Then he asked, "Has Polto come for breakfast?"

"I don't think so."

"Please see if he is alright."

"But my dear, after what he did to you."

"I am worried about him. And I am worried about what made him like that."

"He is not worried about you or he would have come to find out if you are alright."

"Please find out."

Arlaya cried, "No please don't, he may do the same to you. He has obviously gone mad."

"But you can't leave him to starve." Darius sobbed.

Nemroz did not share his compassion for Polto, who had left Darius nearly as bad as the soldiers in the city had. As he had promised Darius, he took some food to the barn. Just called that he had brought some food and left it at the top of the ladder. On the way back to the kitchen he fetched the pail of milk. Then he went to Pops and asked him what he wanted him to do.

"You marry my niece against my wishes, now you expect me to take you back as though nothing had happened."

"But there is no one else to do the work sir."

"Get out and don't come back!"

Arlaya rushed to his side, "Please I beg you no. I will never have another chance to find love."

"How can you love that, he cannot provide for you. He cannot do anything useful."

"He does, he loves me."

"And what use is that?"

She grabbed Nemroz by the hand and ran from the room. "My world is falling apart."

"Sadly Pops is right, I cannot provide for you."

"You work hard and you are learning. You know what is needed in the vegetable field. We can work together."

"I cannot expect you to do that. And what if we were successful last night?"

A sudden look of horror came over her face. And she ran to the cow shed'

Nemroz followed her. "You are all putting me in an impossible position. I want to be with Darius, I want to be with you. I feel I should do the little work I can and I am worried about Polto. I can't see a way out. Life was not supposed to be like this"

"I want to run."

"Where would we go?"

"We could return to father's farm."

"But how could we live? There was nothing left there."

"Just go."

"Do you really want me to go?"

She collapsed at his feet. "No, my darling no. I never knew life could be so complicated."

"Polto should carry out the punishment for what I did last night. It is all my fault."

"No, no, no!" she shouted frantically. "Come we will go to the field and see what needs doing. That is something off your list. It is no help arguing."

Nemroz reluctantly agreed, "We will have to get the tools from the barn."

"But Polto is there."

"You said it is ticking something off the list. I am ticking."

He strode off to the barn. "Are you coming?"

So Arlaya went scurrying after him. Before he collected the tools he went straight to the ladder. The plate of food was still there, so he climbed the ladder. By then Arlaya was there and begging, "No, no."

"Leave this to me. Polto are you there?"

Suddenly he sprang out from behind him. Nemroz swung round. "Polto, what has happened to you? First Darius now me. But do not think you can leave me the way you did Darius." Nemroz grabbed him and threw him to the floor and pinned him there. "I want to know what is going on."

At first Polto was writhing and kicking like a wild animal. But Nemroz held him pinned there.

"Now calm down."

Then suddenly Polto went limp. He sobbed, "You always were stronger than me."

"So you took it out on poor little Darius. What has he ever done to you, except love you?"

"I am sorry. I am sorry."

"It is not me you should be apologizing to. It is Darius. He is in a bad way."

"Will he recover?" Polto sobbed.

"He did not deserve this. He has not long recovered from a bad beating from the soldiers. I nearly lost him. I care if you don't."

"I do still care for him."

"You have a strange way of showing it."

"Will he see me?"

"If he has any sense he won't, but the poor soul still loves you."

Polto just turned away.

"If I let go of you, will you stop this? Or have I got to give YOU a beating?"

"Nemroz what has happened to me?"

"Well, you tell me. This is not the Polto I knew all those years at the temple."

"The temple." He whispered, and lay quivering.

"Polto what's the matter?"

But he did not say any more.

Nemroz asked Arlaya to go and ask if he could take Polto to the cottage, he is not well. Nemroz fetched some water and he slowly helped Polto to sip it.

"Pops has agreed that Polto can be brought to the sitting room, if you can guaranty he is no longer dangerous."

"I am not sure how I can do that. And I am not sure how I am going to get him there."

The water seemed to have calmed Polto. He opened his eyes and gazed at Nemroz, "Did I really hurt Darius?"

"Yes you did."

"Take me to him."

"I can't get you down the ladder. And I could not carry you the way I did Darius."

"Help me, I must get to him."

Polto started struggling towards the ladder. Nemroz helped him, but he was afraid he would fall.

Between the three of them, they got him down the ladder, and with Polto's arms round the shoulders of Nemroz and Arlaya, he struggled to the cottage and straight to the little sitting room. On hearing someone entering the room, Darius slowly opened his eyes. He tried to grin, saying in a faint whisper, "Polto is that you?"

Polto struggled free of his helpers and fell on his knees by Darius sobbing, "My darling, please forgive me."

Darius gazed longingly at him and gasped, "Why?" When he realized Polto was not well he said to Terrace, "Let me lie on the floor, Polto needs the couch."

"No Darius, you are in more need than Polto, and it is his fault you are here."

"Then let Polto lie with me."

"Darius you are wonderful. I didn't even think you would see me."

"Of course I would see you. I am not dead."

Everyone was amazed that Darius did not seem to hold what Polto had done against him. Then Darius realized Nemroz was there too.

He gasped, "What are you doing here? You should be with Arlaya."

"I dare not leave you with Polto."

Polto sobbed, "What have I done? I have hurt my dear Darius, and Nemroz cannot trust me. Take me away."

But Darius sobbed, "No, no, please do not do that. Please let him lie with me. I am sure Polto will not do this again."

"How could I, if my dear friend can still trust me, after what I have done?"

Terrace asked if Polto had eaten and was told, he hadn't. When Polto did not answer, Darius said, Try some milk or some weak broth."

Terrace answered, "We have no broth, I will fetch some milk."

Polto replied, "Please bring some for Darius."

Terrace brought two beakers of milk, Polto said, "Please put them where I can reach, I will help Darius."

Nemroz and Arlaya stayed until the meal was ready, then Nemroz said, "Dare I leave you this time?"

Polto sobbed, "Please trust me."

Nemroz and Arlaya left, collected their meals and took them to the cow shed.

CHAPTER

7

After they had eaten their meal in silence, Nemroz sat gazing at Arlaya

"Are you going to just sit and gaze at me all night?" said Arlaya.

"I want you."

"But you are worried about your friends. Terrace is there. Can you not forget them for just one night?"

"My darling you are making this harder. You know I want you more than anything in the world. Please help me."

She slowly stood and removed her clothes. "Will that help?"

Nemroz gasped and took her hands and led them to the fastening of his clothes.

"That will help more still." Then he lay before her.

To his astonishment she lay on top of him and took the lead.

"My darling you are wonderful. I said help but I did not expect this. This is marvellous."

Nemroz managed better than he had the night before. For one brief marvellous moment he forgot, Darius, the temple, everything except Arlaya.

When he had finished he gasped, "Marriage is better than I had ever dared hope."

"Even if I had to take the lead?"

"Please forgive me. I wish you understood what my mind has to battle with."

"But it was worth it?"

She gave him a great long kiss. They went to sleep in each other's arms.

But in the night Arlaya was woken by Nemroz screaming. She woke him saying, "Is being with me that bad?"

"No my darling, being with you is unbelievably wonderful."

"Then why were you screaming?"

"I would try to tell you, but it would upset you." Then under his breath he added, "Even Darius vomited."

Arlaya looked shocked. "You were not screaming because of what we were doing then?"

"No, I was receiving the punishment for what I have done. Though I hope that in reality I would be brave enough not to scream like that. Though it is very painful."

"But darling there's no one here that will torture you."

"I know you are trying to help." He sobbed. "I am sorry I woke you. I should sleep alone."

"No, please don't do that. I hope in time your pain will ease. Now please hug me."

They did eventually get back to sleep.

The next morning Garetta brought their breakfasts to the cow shed again. After eating it Nemroz insisted he went to the field to work on the vegetables. Arlaya begged to come with him. There was no one now in the barn, so it was safe to collect the tools and they set out for the barn.

At the door Nemroz turned and said, "I must see that Darius is alright first."

Not stopping for Arlaya he rushed to the cottage and to the room where Darius had been taken.

Without stopping to ask, he burst in the room. Darius was lying on the couch in Polto's arms. He gazed up at Nemroz, who asked anxiously, "Have you been alright?"

Darius's voice was very faint so Nemroz knelt beside them.

"I am sure it was a temporary madness. He was so gentle last night. But I am worried about him, he does not seem well."

"I was so worried about you."

"I will heal, but what is the matter with Polto."

"You are unbelievable. You always care more about Polto, no matter what he does to you."

"I don't matter."

"You do to me."

"Oh, Nemroz. I am sorry may I call you that?"

At that moment Arlaya caught up with Nemroz. "Is Darius alright?"

Darius answered for him, "I am fine. Were you and Nemroz good last night?"

Arlaya ignored the nightmare and said, "He is wonderful."

At that moment Terrace joined them, carrying two beakers of milk. She explained, Darius is still very weak and Polto will take nothing but milk.

Darius turned back to Nemroz, "I will be alright, Terrace will look after us."

Nemroz replied, "Can I come back to see you later?"

"I would love that. Next to Polto, you mean the most to me in the world."

Feeling a little emotional he stood, took Arlaya by the hand and left.

"Now we really must get some work done. The maids will run out of vegetables."

"But Pops has told you to get out."

"All the more reason for me to work hard."

"At the temple they did some terrible things, but they bred some amazing individuals."

They worked in the field each day. And Arlaya gave the vegetables to Garetta to take to the maids. Garetta brought meals to the cow shed and Terrace took care of Polto and Darius.

CHAPTER

One day when Nemroz and Arlaya were working in the field, Arlaya called out, "Nemroz I saw someone in the meadow beyond the hedge. There is no one working in that field anymore."

Fearing there was danger, Nemroz said, "You stay there, I will go and see."

"Do be careful."

Nemroz walked to the hedge and cautiously peered over. There staggering alone was a stranger, dressed like the priest in the city. Nemroz feared what would happen to his friends, but he felt he could not just leave this man. He went through the gap in the hedge and approached him. By the time he reached him he had collapsed. Nemroz bent down to him. First he tried his own language, then when he did not understand, he tried to remember some of the words from the priest's language. The stranger looked up in astonishment, but used more words than Nemroz could understand.

Nemroz reached down and helped him to his feet. He put his arm round his shoulder and tried to help the shuffling man to walk. As soon as Arlaya saw them coming, she rushed to help. Between them, in stages, they eventually got him as far as the yard. Nemroz sent Arlaya to fetch Garetta and Terrace. The four of them discussed what they should do. Nemroz explained that although the priests had travelled with the invaders, they had helped him and his friends. It was decided they should help the priest. Terrace went to check who was in the kitchen, then called them to bring him in. They took him to the room where Polto and Darius were. Polto looked furious, but Darius looked scared.

But Nemroz said, "Alright calm down, we could not just leave him out there."

It was decided that, since Darius was so much better now, he and Polto should return to the barn and the stranger should be tended in the room.

Darius was not sure about that, he said to Polto. "You know all I want is to be with you. But can I trust you? I could not survive another beating."

Polto openly wept saying, "Oh, I would never want to hurt you, please help me."

Darius became quite overcome. He took Polto by the hand and led him to the barn. Once they were up the ladder he said, "I am glad that happened, now I can lie with you."

"My dearest Darius, can you trust me?"

Darius just gazed longingly at him for a while before saying, "I just want things to be as they were, but you seem different."

Polto glared at him.

Darius started shaking, "Please don't hit me!"

Polto was breathing deeply, trying to control his emotions.

Meanwhile in the cottage Terrace agreed to look after the priest.

But she said, "How will I communicate with him?"

Nemroz said, "I know a little of his language, and I am sure he will soon learn ours. Please start by bringing him some water.

Then to Arlaya he said, There is no time to return to the field now. We will return to the shed after the meal."

The water did seem to revive the priest a little. Nemroz started sharing some words until the priest fell asleep. Nemroz and Arlaya had their meal in the room, while Garetta and Terrace ate theirs in the kitchen. Then when Terrace returned, Nemroz said, "When he wakes try him with some food. Arlaya and I are returning to the shed."

When they were safely in the shed, Arlaya said. "If we lie together again tonight will that give you nightmares again?"

"Oh my darling, I wish you understood, it is not because I don't want you. I want you very, very much. I wish I could control the pain in my mind when I am asleep." He whispered under his breath, "It is painful for me too."

"Would it help if we do not do it tonight?"

"No, my love I need you, and I don't expect it would help anyway. Please forgive me if I wake you up. I certainly do not want to."

They were intimate together and Nemroz was finding it easier now, and even more enjoyable. But he still had the dreadful nightmares.

Next morning, even before Garetta came with the breakfasts, Nemroz said, "I must see if Darius is alright. He rushed to the barn. Shouting before he reached the ladder, "Darius are you alright?"

A sleepy Darius came to the edge of the gallery, "Yes, we were fine. It was wonderful to lie with Polto again."

Nemroz was so relieved. "Do you want some breakfast?"

"I do. Can I have it here? Wait I will see if Polto does."

But when he returned he was not so sure. "Polto only wants some milk. I am not sure I should have any."

"If you want breakfast, you have breakfast. You need building up."

Not waiting for the girls, Nemroz strode across to the kitchen and fetched a breakfast and two beakers of milk. He had several hostile stairs, but no one dared stop him. As he entered the barn he called, "Can you fetch Polto's milk?"

Darius came and fetched it, then returned for his own.

Nemroz said quietly, "Will you come down?" Darius looked round nervously, then came quietly down.

"Come sit with me."

Darius reluctantly followed Nemroz. They sat among the old equipment.

"Here eat your breakfast. I am worried about you with Polto."

"Polto did not harm me."

"Not this time. Yet you were still worried to eat breakfast."

"That was me being silly."

"I don't think so, he is still acting very strangely."

"I want to be with him. Anyway I have nowhere else to go."

"You could return to the cottage."

"I would be no safer with the priest, and I love being with Polto."

"I cannot risk him harming you again."

"What happens to me doesn't matter."

"It does to me."

"That is very kind, but you have Arlaya."

"Yes, I love Arlaya, you know what it is like to love someone, but I have known you longer than Arlaya and you mean a lot to me."

"That means more to me than you can imagine. But I need to be with Polto, even if he kills me."

"No, it is too dangerous, I am not prepared to risk that."

Nemroz picked him up and carried him like a child and carried him first to the shed.

Arlaya looked shocked saying, "What are you doing?"

"I cannot risk leaving Darius with Polto. Polto is not responsible for his actions. We will have to find another solution. When we have had breakfast, I will try to communicate with the priest."

Darius sat there sobbing, "No, please don't."

Twice while they waited for Garetta he tried to run for the door, but Nemroz pulled him back.

"The last thing I would ever want to do is to use violence on you of all people. But you must stop this. It is not safe for you to be with Polto."

"But this will be a torment to me, and I think Polto still wants me."

Nemroz did not tell Darius what he thought, it would hurt Darius too much.

Then Garetta came with the breakfast. Darius dared not defy Nemroz.

He sat there shaking and sobbing. "Please don't make me leave Polto."

"Only for now."

When they had eaten, Nemroz turned again to Darius, "Are you coming voluntarily, or do I have to carry you again?"

Darius admitted that it had hurt from where Polto hit him when Nemroz had carried him. So he rose and walked toward the door.

"I will come too." Arlaya insisted

Nemroz was not happy about that. But he did not stop her. Nemroz held Darius's hand and he walked calmly to the cottage, not speaking, he walked to the room where the priest was.

Terrace looked surprised at their return. Not explaining, Nemroz indicated for the priest to sit up and told Darius to sit on the couch. Poor Darius looked more scared of the priest than he ever was of Polto. Nemroz turned to Terrace saying. "I need to work in the field this morning. Take care of them for me, I will be back later." And to Arlaya, "I think it would be best if you stay here and support Terrace." He left and went to the barn and collected the tools.

He worked until about mid-day, collected up some vegetables and the tools. While in the barn he called up to Polto, who did not reply, so he climbed the ladder. Polto was lying with his face to the wall. Nemroz crossed the gallery and rolled Polto over. "Are you not going to talk to me?"

He lay there and glared at him. "Why should I?"

"At the moment others need me, but I will be back later and I want an explanation to all this. So you had better be thinking about it." Nemroz turned and left.

He took the vegetables to the kitchen, then went to see the others. He asked Arlaya if they had been alright. "I have been talking to Terrace. Neither of them has said anything."

Nemroz asked Darius why he had been silent.

Darius replied, "I can't speak his language, and I would not risk being hurt if I could."

Arlaya looked puzzled, "Do you know this man?"

Not this man, but one just like him." Showing the great pain he felt.

Arlaya looked away saying, "Why did you three come here bringing all your hurt?"

That tore Nemroz's heart.

Nemroz shuddered, then sat on the floor beside the priest and made a start with conveying their language.

They worked until it was time for the meal. Nemroz said to Arlaya, "You have your meal, I must take something to Polto. I told him I would come back to talk to him. I will see you in the shed later." He collected some food from the kitchen and left for the barn.

Polto still did not answer when he called, so he took the food up to the gallery. Polto was still facing the wall.

Nemroz swung him round and sat him up, "Now this is not good enough, you must have something to eat."

"Why, no one cares ."

"That is not fair. Darius is pining his heart out for you. And I am here aren't I?"

"You have Arlaya, and I would rather have you than him."

"Ah, now we are getting to the truth. You have never accepted that I am not like you. You resent that I love Arlaya. That is not fair to me, and it is very cruel to Darius. Poor soul, he still adores you, even after all you have done to him. You sent him to me. He always did his best for me. But it was only for your sake. Why can't you accept things as they are? Darius is the only one who can love you as you are, and he is such a wonderful person." At first Nemroz thought Polto was going to fly into a rage, but then he just collapsed into great sobs. Nemroz through his arms round him.

"Why can't you love me?" he sobbed.

Nemroz replied softly, "I do not love the way you and Darius do, you know that."

"This is driving me mad."

"I can see that. What can I do to help?"

"I want you not Darius."

"That is very selfish. If you keep this up none of us will be happy. You seemed to be happy with Darius when we were in the city."

"But you were there then."

"Do you not want me to be happy?"

Polto through his arms round Nemroz and sobbed uncontrollably.

"I must go now. If I can't trust you not to hurt Darius, you will have to stay alone. You think about it. And eat the food. I will see you tomorrow."

Polto was too distraught to stop him. Nemroz just left.

He stopped outside and lent against the door while he collected himself thinking, 'Why can't I just be with Arlaya.' He went to the shed and was so relieved when Arlaya was there. He fell at her feet saying, "Why can't they all just go away? I just want to be with you."

Arlaya looked so sad and she said, "You're with me now, just hold me."

"Is life always so complicated? I thought once I did not have the responsibilities of the temple, that life would be simple."

"My dear Nemroz they all expect too much from you. Just lie with me and forget them all."

Next morning Nemroz went to see if Darius was alright. When he entered the little room he could not see Darius, and in fear he cried, "Darius where are you?"

A weak voice came from behind the couch.

"What are you doing down there?"

Darius crawled out crying, "I would have been beaten if I lay with the priest."

"Oh my dear friend, come and help me teach the priest our language. I do not think he would hurt you."

"I am not safe anywhere. Please protect me."

When the priest realised Darius had slept on the floor, the next night he insisted that since it was Darius that was hurt, it was Darius who should have the couch. Darius dared not argue.

After that Nemroz spent each morning in the field and each afternoon teaching the priest their language, but Darius would not help.

In time with Terrace's patient care Darius recovered enough to help in the field. Nemroz tried to spend what time he could with Polto, but he still seemed very distracted and he hardly ate and would not leave the barn. Nemroz still did not trust him to be with Darius. And Darius was very unhappy.

Each night Nemroz would spend with Arlaya. They still enjoyed their intimacy and there were only a few nights when Nemroz had the nightmare about the punishment.

One day when Darius was working with Nemroz in the field. Nemroz returned for his time with the priest. Darius said he would continue in the field. As soon as Nemroz was out of sight, Darius went straight to the barn. He was distraught to find that Polto did not even want to see him. It was not until Nemroz and Arlaya returned to the shed at mealtime that they found Darius in a heap sobbing his heart out. Nemroz put his arms round him saying, "My dear fellow. What is the matter?"

"I went to Polto." He sobbed.

Alarmed Nemroz replied, "Did he hurt you?"

"No worse, he would not see me."

"Polto is very cruel."

"Please do not send me back to the priest. He won't except me. I still want Polto. Please help me."

It was Arlaya who responded, "You poor thing, life is so unfair."

Darius gazed pleadingly at Nemroz, "What you do with Arlaya is not that different to what I did with Polto. Please let me stay here. I promise I will stay hidden." Then he added, "I am so unhappy, no one wants me." Nemroz turned to Arlaya, "I do not want to throw him out, he did so much for me in the temple days."

"Just for tonight, if he stays in the cow stall, I don't want to know he is here."

"I would love to be with Nemroz, but I promise I will stay hidden out of sight." Which is what he did.

Next morning they found him sobbing, "No one wants me, I want to die."

Nemroz fell on top of him and sobbed too.

Arlaya muttered, "I can't cope with you males who cry like babies."

Nemroz did not wait for Garetta to bring breakfast. He walked in the kitchen and fetched one and took it straight to the barn. He did not stop to call to Polto. He climbed the ladder and went straight to where Polto lay. He grabbed hold of him and sat him up.

Staring him in the face he said, "This has got to stop."

"What has?" Polto said sleepily.

"Being so cruel to Darius."

"Why what has the silly little squirt done now?"

"Is that what you think of him? You cruel, selfish…. Thing. It is just as well you are no longer a priest. You are not fit to be one. If you do not make it up with Darius, I will throw you out."

"You have no authority here."

"Maybe not, but I will throw you out just the same. You are an idiot, Darius is the only chance of comfort you have. I found him a comfort, and I am not like you two. You make it up with Darius, or you leave. And if you ever hurt him, I will kill you."

Polto had never realized he was afraid of Nemroz, but he had never seen him like that.

"Bring him to me." He whimpered.

"No, you eat that breakfast, then come with me."

It worked, he obediently ate the food, then followed Nemroz down the ladder.

They went to the cow shed and found Arlaya comforting Darius.

"What have you to say to Darius."

"Please forgive me, but I don't expect you would want to come back to me."

"Of course I want to come back to you. Do you really mean you will take me?" Darius said, looking longingly at Polto.

"Do you want to go to the barn?" Nemroz prompted.

Polto took Darius by the hand and led him to the door.

Nemroz said, "Now you remember what I said."

On the way to the barn Darius asked, "Do you really want me?"

"Please forgive me. I have not been in my right mind."

Then as they got to the door Darius hesitated and asked, "Are you going to hurt me?"

"Oh my darling, I am so sorry. All this should never have happened to you. Let me show you how much I want you."

"Are you sure?"

"Oh, how can I have done this to you. I want to show you that you can trust me again."

And gently held out his hand to him. Poor Darius was torn by a longing for closeness and a fear of what had happened before.

Nemroz was nervous all day, worried whether Darius was safe. Arlaya had to restrain him from going to check upon them saying, "They need their privacy, leave them be."

He found it hard to settle to anything. But he did spend time working with the priest.

They were all surprised and relieved when Polto and Darius arrived for their meal in the evening looking safe and happy. They were all amazed they had spent all day together. Arlaya was almost jealous.

Next morning they came to breakfast as well. Garetta told them to go to the cow shed after breakfast.

Nemroz was so pleased to see them. "Are you two well enough to join me in the field now?"

Polto looked surprised, "I thought Pops had not wanted you to return to the field."

"Someone had to do the work. We need the vegetables to eat."

"I did a little while you were unwell." Said Darius enthusiastically.

The three of them set out together as they had when they first came. Pops still did not know it was Nemroz working the field.

Polto felt a little weak, it was so long since he had been outside. They worked together tending the vegetables and collecting those that were ready.

Then about mid-day Nemroz said, "In the afternoon I usually work with the priest."

"Who is that?" Polto snarled.

"While you were unwell someone joined us."

"Who was that? Who is he?"

Darius stood watching Polto nervously.

We found him in the field. He was in a bad way." Nemroz explained.

"They made me share a room with him."

"Why was that a problem? Why will neither of you tell me who he is?"

"He is one of the foreign priests." Said Nemroz cautiously.

"How could you!" Polto roared.

Nemroz calmly replied, "It was the priest who rescued you both in the city, and it was not him who hurt you."

"It was his doctrine and his followers." Polto growled.

Nothing more was said until they were back in the yard. When they had put the tools away in the barn, Nemroz asked, "Well what are you two doing?"

Darius looked nervously at Polto, who eventually said, "There is no way I am going to see this…"

To Nemroz he said, "You be careful, do not mention us."

Nemroz replied. "You be careful, take good care of Darius."

Nemroz was still nervous about leaving Darius with Polto. He went to the cottage and spent some time with the priest. When it was time for the evening meal, Terrace brought one for the priest. Arlaya came with her and she asked Nemroz if he was prepared to have his meal in the kitchen.

"Pops will not allow that."

"Please come and see, Pops knows you are still here."

Thinking there was probably nothing Pops could physically do, as he knew they were all on his side he followed Arlaya. He found they had left his old seat for him. Everyone but Pops greeted him, asking him to join them.

After the meal Nemroz held out his hand and they left.

"I told you it would be fine."

"Can we just forget them all? I just want to lie with you."

They walked back to the shed.

He just reached out to undo her fastenings. "I wish I could spend more time with you, but I am so glad to have you to myself now."

"Oh my darling, just make the world go away."

That night he did not even have the nightmare.

CHAPTER

As Arlaya's pregnancy became more advanced, Nemroz insisted she no longer came with them to the field. Often it was Arlaya and Garetta who sat with the priest while the other three worked in the field. As Arlaya's time came near, Terrace insisted that room must be found for them in the cottage. She said, "A cow shed was not suitable for having a baby."

Pops reluctantly agreed, and some rearrangements were made. By then Pops's legs had got worse. And he had great difficulty climbing to the upper floor. The priest was moved into the servants' quarters. The room downstairs was turned into a bedroom for Pops and Nemroz and Arlaya moved into the main bedroom on the upper floor.

That night Arlaya led Nemroz to their new quarters. They climbed what was little more substantial than the ladder to the hayloft, to the upper floor, to a reasonable sized room, with a double bed and a trunk for clothes etc. Nemroz had never slept in a double bed. The nearest he had ever had to a proper bed was the bunk in the early days at the temple. He stood and gazed around the room.

"Is this for us? Can this be real?"

"You are my husband, it is only right we have a room like this."

He whispered, "Is it right that I should be a husband?"

Arlaya removed her clothes, folding them and laying them on the trunk. When she turned back to Nemroz he was still standing there in a trance.

"Are you coming?" Arlaya said softly.

Nemroz turned his trance like gaze to Arlaya saying, "Please help me."

Arlaya fumbled with his fastenings. Then Nemroz lifted her onto the bed.

He gently stroked her growing belly saying, "You take control, I don't want to hurt you."

She kissed him and mounted him. He did respond to her, but oh so gently.

When they had done, Arlaya slipped back down beside him. "You are so different to the men round here."

He gazed at her saying, "I try so hard. I wear their clothes and I am learning to work in the fields."

"That is good, people are beginning to accept you now, but I never want you to change. You are more gentle and caring than anyone I have ever known."

Nemroz threw his arms round her and kissed her, and they went to sleep in each other's arms.

But in the night Arlaya was woken by Nemroz screaming.

She woke him saying, "It's alright. It is one of your nightmares." He looked sleepily at her. "It's alright Nemroz, you are safe in your new bed with me. I do wish there was some way I could help. Why can you not tell me about the temple?"

"I tried, but it was too painful to remember."

"Is there no one who could help?"

"There is... But that would be too risky. I could not risk hurting him, he has suffered too much."

Arlaya left it there saying, "Come relax, let's get back to sleep."

Next morning Arlaya was awake first, and lay thinking about what had been said during the night. Nemroz had started to say there was someone who could help with this problem about the temple. Who had suffered more than anyone else, and knew about the temple? Surely that must be Darius. Would she dare ask him?

It was some time before there was an opportunity for Arlaya to be alone with Darius.

She cautiously approached him. "Can I have a word with you?"

"Why what is the matter?"

"Nemroz has problems with memories of the temple."

"Well you should ask him."

"I have, it is too painful for him to tell me. Can you tell me what happened?"

Darius looked away. "It is not for me to tell you."

"Please, it tortures him. Please help."

Darius winced and shook. "I am not sure I can either." He whimpered.

"Was it things you did, or things he did?"

"It was things he had to do. Now leave it please." And he ran off.

That night when Nemroz and Arlaya where settled in bed, Arlaya asked, "What did you do when you were High Priest at the temple?"

"I have told you, I prepared the offerings."

"But there is something else, that was much more painful for you."

"Please leave it." He was near to tears.

"My dear Nemroz I need you to tell me. Only then can I understand and hopefully help you."

Suddenly he said, "Did you ask Darius?"

Arlaya looked bashful.

"Darling how could you? What did he tell you?"

"Only that it was something you had to do."

"Please do not upset him anymore. If I told you, it would upset you too, and that is not necessary."

"But then at least I could understand."

"You never give up do you."

"No, because I love you. And even if I cannot help, at least you would not hurt alone."

Nemroz sobbed, "Give me the courage to tell you if I must."

He told her about the punishment and why. About the sword blows, about the staunching the blood and that they were surrendered to Farago with no wine to help the pain.

Arlaya through her arms around him and sobbed.

"You would not believe me that it would upset you."

"At least I now understand your pain. Especially if they were priests you knew."

Nemroz could hold his composure no longer and they sobbed together. After some time she gazed at him, "And you think that should happen to you?"

"Now you understand."

"But the temple has been destroyed. No one here would hurt you."

"Maybe I should hurt myself, no one took over from me."

"No my darling. Do not even think such a thing. We are to have a child soon, they will need a father."

"Arlaya just come to me. Please help me."

A few nights later Nemroz asked, "How are you getting on with the priest?"

"Very well now. He has learnt a lot of our language."

"And what has he told you?"

"That his name is Arken."

"And what else?"

"He mostly asks questions."

"What has he told you of where he comes from and what he believes?"

"You sound suspicious."

"It is just that I met his sort in the city, and Polto and Darius got hurt. Now he is better we should send him on his way."

"But now he is better he could be helpful."

"He has nothing to offer."

"We accepted you, I am ashamed of you."

"Now he is beginning to talk like us, I am worried he will talk to Polto and Darius."

"Why to those two in particular? Why are you three such a problem?"

"The beliefs of the priest in the city were a great problem for them. It was because they got so hurt that we had to escape from the city. If they have to run again, I will have to lose them or lose you."

Arlaya looked shocked and frightened. "There is always a problem with you priests. Why did I fall in love with you in the first place?"

"My darling, this priest, Arken did you say his name is? Must go before he talks to Polto."

"Darling he has done no wrong."

"No, not yet."

"Please forget it and come to bed."

"Why is life always so difficult?"

"I am sure a lot of the time it is because you make it so. Take your clothes off and come and hold me."

Nemroz did, but he could not help worrying.

Next morning. While dressing Arlaya asked Nemroz to speak to Arken. "Surely it would be better to solve the problem, than to lose another helper."

"I would not be able to change his beliefs." Nemroz said abruptly, and went to breakfast.

Arlaya went to speak to Arken before she joined him.

After breakfast Arken came and said, "I understand you want to speak to me."

Nemroz glared at Arlaya, then followed Arken into the yard.

"Shall we go to my quarters?"

Nemroz reluctantly followed. It was a bare room with just a bed. Arken offered Nemroz a seat on the bed.

"Do the girls share your bed?" he scowled.

"No we sit on the floor."

Nemroz started with noncommittal questions about the language progress etc., then he asked "Would your beliefs be the same as the priests who travelled with the army?"

"I do not know any personally, but I expect so."

"I studied with one for some time in the city."

"That is interesting. How did you get on?"

"I was interested in a lot of what he had to say, but he was very cruel to some friends of mine."

"That is very unlike one of us."

So Nemroz asked straight out, "What is your teaching about relationships?"

"In what way?" Arken replied guardedly.

"Who should have relations with whom?" Nemroz asked bluntly.

Arken paused, then answered cautiously. "Are you referring to a married man and woman?"

"And what if a man is devoted to a man?"

Arken stopped and eyed Nemroz up and down, fearing trouble. "That should not be a problem for you, you have a beautiful wife."

"Maybe, answer my question."

"Please ask the person to whom this applies to speak to me."

That caught Nemroz out, there was no way he would risk his friends being hurt again. Then recovering, he said, "Would such a person be accepted into your fellowship?"

That caught Arken off guard, "That depends on whether he acts on that devotion."

"Then I will have to ask you to leave."

Arken stared at Nemroz startled. "You do not have that authority here."

"Do you wish to challenge that?"

"Now wait a minute, this is not necessary."

"It certainly is, I will not have my friends crushed again."

"I am sure you are (he muttered as he did not know the word).

"I am not exaggerating." Nemroz prompted. "My friends were beaten up and abused."

"Do you think I would be capable of that, even if I wanted to?"

"I want a firm undertaking that you will accept my friends and you will treat them as reasonable people."

"You mean Polto and Darius don't you?"

"Maybe. I do not want you here."

"As I remember, it was you who brought me in."

"I could not leave you to die. You're better now. Take your doctrine to the city."

"I only wish to repay you for your kindness."

"By telling my friends they are filthy and disgusting."

"I would not do that. I may try to help them, but would never be unkind. I can promise that."

Nemroz glared at him. Arken just said, "You can trust me."

"We'll see." And Nemroz walked out.

He went to find Polto and Darius and the three of them went to the field.

At the meal that evening Arlaya was waiting for Nemroz.

"You didn't have to tackle Arken like that."

"You forced my hand. You had said deal with the problem. Anyway, how did you know what happened?"

"Well."

"Arken came running to you."

"Don't be cross."

"He probably twisted everything."

"We will talk about it later, alright? Sit down."

Nemroz did not say anymore.

Later when they were getting ready for bed Arlaya pleaded, "Please don't let us fight."

"You know that is the last thing I want, but I have to defend my friends."

"Can they not defend themselves?"

"You saw the state Polto was in, and what he did to Darius."

"You always have to fight for everyone."

"You said you don't want me to change."

"You win, come to bed. But be gentle."

"I am always gentle, I love you."

CHAPTER

A few days later Nemroz decided to risk speaking to Polto and Darius about Arken. When they were walking to the field together, Nemroz began, "I am worried about this priest, Arken he calls himself, spending so much time in his quarters with the girls."

The other two looked concerned, but offered no solution.

"I think it is about time he helped with the work, if he is to stay."

Polto retorted, "But he is a priest like the ones in the city isn't he? There is no way I am working with him."

"Give him a chance."

"Why should I? Have you forgotten what they did to us?"

"He has promised he will not hurt you."

Polto rounded on him furiously, "Have you spoken to him about us? How dare you?"

Darius backed away terrified.

"Calm down Polto, you're frightening Darius."

"It is not me he needs to be frightened of, it is this so called priest."

"When you have calmed down, I want you both to speak to him."

Nemroz decided to take charge of the situation. He had long ago wanted to join this new religious group. It had only been their attitude to his friends that had stopped him. Before the evening meal he asked Arken if they could come to his quarters next morning. Nemroz did not say anymore that night, not even to Arlaya.

Next day as the three of then entered the yard after breakfast Nemroz announced we are not going straight to the field. The other two followed him not realizing what was happening. The next thing they knew, they were sitting on the floor in Arken's room.

Nemroz looked straight at Arken and said, "Now, I want you to tell my friends that you care for them, and then start explaining this new deity of yours."

At first Polto and Darius just looked stunned, then Polto flew into a rage, and Darius looked terrified. Nemroz had difficulty persuading him not to run.

Once Arken recovered his breath, he decided it was safer to comply. Darius edged closer to Nemroz and whispered, "Does he mean it?"

Nemroz replied, "I am sure he does. He knows he has me to answer to if he doesn't."

When things calmed down Arken began to explain the things the priest in the city had explained to Nemroz when he was working on the translations. How this new deity was the creator of the whole world and the whole universe. How He cared for all mankind and He wanted them to respond to Him. That mankind had gone astray. Nemroz announced they would leave it there and come back tomorrow. Even Polto dared not challenge Nemroz when he was in that mood. The three left and went to the field.

Both Polto and Darius were very subdued. When Darius found himself out of Polto's earshot he asked Nemroz, if he could talk to him alone.

Nemroz replied, "When Polto goes to the kitchen, go to the cow shed and I will join you there."

They were both relieved when they managed that.

"My dear master, there are two things I am worried about. The priest has not said about me and Polto. Will he say I am bad? And I am scared when Polto gets in a rage."

"Arken, the priest cannot by himself attack you, as you were in the city. What he will say I can't guaranty. As for Polto, I am more worried about that. I am worried how stable he is now. Are you scared to stay with him? I do not know where else you can go."

"Do you think he would hurt me again? I always prefer to be with Polto, but I am scared I would not survive another beating."

"My dear Darius what have I done to you? I was worried what Arken would do, so I brought him into the open. I have warned him. I am sure he doesn't mean you any harm."

"If only you were not with Arlaya you could protect me."

"Please never resent me being with Arlaya. I could not bear that from you."

"Believe me I don't, but I am scared."

"Would you be safer with Arken?"

"Please don't make me do that."

"What can I do for you?"

"You came to me. I welcomed you. Why can you not protect me?"

"Oh my dear Darius you are tearing me in two."

Darius fell at his feet and sobbed, "I am sorry."

"Come let us go for the meal. We will see how Polto is. Perhaps we should talk with him afterwards."

They entered the kitchen and sat in their usual seats. At first Polto glared at Darius "Would you rather be with Nemroz?"

"You know I would always rather be with you, but I get scared when you fly into a rage."

"I am sorry, I will not hurt you. Please be with me."

After the meal Darius quietly followed Polto to the barn.

When Arlaya and Nemroz settled for the night she asked, what was going on.

You told me to sort things with Arken. I am not sure whether I am helping or making things worse."

"I am sure you are doing your best."

"I am worried Darius will get hurt again. He asked me to protect him. How can I do that?"

"I feel sorry for your little friend, but he is not sleeping in here."

Next morning when they went to breakfast, Polto and Darius were not there. Breakfast was finished and they still had not arrived. Nemroz went across to the barn. He called from the bottom of the ladder. There was a shuffle from the gallery and Darius appeared.

Nemroz rushed up the ladder and helped him down. Darius had a nasty black eye and a wound on his throat.

"What have you done to him." Nemroz roared.

He climbed the ladder and dragged Polto down. "I told you what I would do if you hurt him again."

Before Nemroz could strike Polto, Darius fell at his feet begging him not to hurt him. Nemroz gazed down at him saying, "How can you defend him? He will kill you one day."

Polto pleaded, "I did not mean to hurt him."

"Then I will not mean to kill you." Nemroz growled.

Darius rose between them pleading, "No please, no."

"You would defend him, but you do not defend yourself."

"It does not matter what happens to me, but I could not survive without Polto."

Nemroz glared at Polto shouting, "I hope you appreciate what you have in Darius." Then through him to the floor adding, "I will let you live this time."

Before he had time to say anything else a knock came on the barn door, one of the maids entered saying. "Your wife's pains have started."

He ran from the barn.

The maid ran after him calling, "Garetta and Terrace are with her, you are not to go up there sir."

He got as far as the bottom of the step ladder before she managed to stop him.

"Please sir, you must not go up. We will tell you as soon as there is any news."

Nemroz was distraught, forgetting all about his friends, he refused to move from the bottom of the step ladder.

He was still there when it came to mealtime. He could not face eating. When his friends did not come to the kitchen, Nemroz suddenly thought, 'Darius. Was he safe?" And he ran back to the barn. They were nowhere to be seen. Nemroz frantically called, "Darius where are you?"

Darius replied, "It's all right I am here." And he came to the edge of the gallery.

"Are you coming to eat?"

"How is Arlaya?"

"They will not let me go to her. Please come to the kitchen with me."

"If Polto will come."

They soon both appeared dressed and descended the ladder. The maids were pleased they came for their meal, but none of them ate much. After the meal there was still no news.

One of the maids asked if Nemroz would be with his friends. She said, "We will call you when there is some news."

Nemroz looked questioningly at Polto. "Yes of course you can."

All three returned to the barn.

"Are you going to join us sir?" Darius said with a bow.

Darius followed Polto up the ladder, but Nemroz was less jovial. Polto and Darius undressed and lay in the hay. Darius giggled and called, "Are you going to be a High Priest for me?"

Nemroz quickly lay beside him as he was, whispering, "Be quiet you will make Polto jealous."

"I heard that. I will not hurt him. It is more than my life's worth."

Darius just gave him a playful kick. Nemroz was glad of the company, but he could not sleep.

It was nearly time for breakfast before Nemroz heard a quiet knock on the door. Nemroz slid down the ladder without waking his two sleeping friends.

The maid quietly said, "You have a son sir."

Forgetting to be quiet Nemroz said excitedly, "Can I go to her now?"

"Come with me." the maid replied.

He nearly flue up the ladder and rushed to Arlaya's side, kneeling by the bed. He gazed at Arlaya saying, "Have we really got a son? I cannot believe I could make a son."

Arlaya showed him the little bundle and he kissed him on the head saying, "I never got to see them as small as that." Then he grinned at Arlaya shyly and said, "What happens now?"

"I will stay here for now. You can work if you like, it is not normal for you to come to me yet."

"But I want to stay with you."

Arlaya gently said, "You will not be able to lie with me for a while."

"Not even if I do not touch you?"

"That is not allowed sir."

"Nemroz can be trusted. Please leave us for a while."

The other women looked very unwilling. But Nemroz insisted he could be trusted not to touch her and without undressing he slid in beside her.

"I will rest shortly, but please let me have some time with Nemroz."

Reluctantly they left. The maid said bluntly, "Only talk mind."

As soon as they were gone Nemroz asked, "Can I not even put my arm round you?" "Of course you can, but gently."

"Oh my darling I never really believed we could make a baby."

"Now don't go getting your nightmares again."

"I am so glad you understand me now. But I did not come to talk about me. How are you and how is our son?"

"I am tired, but the baby is fine."

"Please rest. I will just stay and hold you."

After a few minutes he said, "Pass me the child, you get some sleep."

"But Nemroz!"

"Don't you trust me."

"Of course I do but, what do you know about babies?"

"Only what I knew when I was small, but we were not sent to priest's school until we were about ten. Most of the babies had no parents from very young. I cannot feed him, but I can hold him."

"Nemroz you are amazing."

When the women returned they were horrified to find Arlaya asleep and the baby in Nemroz's arms.

The maid sat on the trunk glaring at Nemroz. She had never seen a man holding a baby before, Garetta suddenly said, "The cow has not been milked!"

Terrace replied, "You go ahead I will stay with Arlaya."

Nemroz added, "When the pail is full get Polto to carry it for you. Then tell them to work in the field. Say I say so." Garetta left.

Nemroz turned to the maid saying, I am sure you have work to do as well. Terrace will call you if there is a problem."

With a disgruntled swirl she left.

Arlaya slept until the baby cried. Terrace was about to help, when Nemroz gently laid him to Arlaya's breast. Terrace was astounded, Nemroz seemed to know how to do that better than she did.

Arlaya gazed at him, "Thankyou, you can tell me later how you know things like that."

Nemroz spent the whole day with Arlaya. When it came to the evening he said. "I will bring Arlaya her meal up to her. You can go and have yours with the others."

Garetta looked nervously at Arlaya. She answered with, "I will be fine, we can trust Nemroz."

Garetta was reluctant to leave.

Nemroz said, "You have seen I know a bit about babies, and you can trust me not to hurt Arlaya."

Nemroz fetched both their meals up to the bedroom. He asked, "Does the baby stay with you all the time?"

"He has a little bed down here."

Nemroz came round, took the bundle, (though she had to show him how to support the baby's head, as Nemroz was not used to them as young as that), and he laid him in the cot.

When they had finished their meal Arlaya asked, "Where did you learn about babies?"

"I was brought up with women and babies until I was at least 10. Most of the babies did not have either parent from an early age."

"I am so glad that terrible place no longer exists."

"It was not that bad. It was all I knew."

Before she thought, she said, "The memory of it gives you nightmares."

Nemroz looked away and said, "Only one thing."

"Oh, Nemroz I'm sorry."

"Forget it. Have you finished with the plate?"

When he returned he slipped back in beside her and asked, "Do you trust me to stay overnight?"

"Can you cope?"

"Should I ask Garetta to stay?"

"If you think it would be safer for now. But I do trust you."

Garetta was not happy, but Arlaya insisted.

In the night, when the baby cried Nemroz said, "Wait I will pass him up to you."

Several nights Nemroz just lay beside her. But it was getting harder each night.

"Can I lie with you the way I did that first night?"

"I would rather you didn't. This is why you were told not to stay with me."

"How much longer will you make me wait?"

"I am sure I will want you soon. I am still sore."

"Please let me just press up against you."

"Please just go to sleep. Please be patient with me."

"I will try, I am only human. Will you be upset if some nights I am not with you?"

"I always like you being here, especially when you help me with the baby. But I understand if that is too much for you."

Nemroz was very sad, but he said no more.

The next morning Arlaya said, "We must find a name for our son."

"As I suggested the other day, I would like it to be Roz, as I was called as a child."

"Does it have to be a name from your past?"

"He is my son as well and he is male, so he should be named after me."

"All right we will inform the family today. He should be named when I first come down, and that should be in the next couple of days."

"I am glad to see you seem to be a little better this morning. When I go down for the breakfasts I want to have a word with Polto."

"Why is that?"

"I must go to the field, I am not sure that Polto and Darius have been tending the vegetables."

Arlaya whispered under her breath, "Pops was crazy to try to send you away."

Nemroz waited until everyone was in for breakfast before he went down. He went straight up to Polto and asked. "How is the vegetable field coming on?"

But it was Darius who admitted, they had not been going to the field.

Though Nemroz was not pleased, he just said. "When you have eaten your breakfast, just wait here."

He took the breakfasts and returned to Arlaya.

Arlaya had only just started her breakfast, when her young son started demanding his. Nemroz came round and picked him up, telling him he would have to learn to be more accommodating.

When Nemroz had finished his breakfast he said, "I must go down now. I will see you later. I will get Garetta or Terrace to come and sit with you."

He collected the other two on the way out. And they went to the field.

When they had finished the work for the day and were walking back to the cottage Nemroz said, looking rather hurt, "Why can't I rely on you two to work without me chasing you?"

Darius said, looking very ashamed, "I am sorry, we will do better."

But Polto just grunted, "We are not your servants."

As they got to the cottage Nemroz added, "Tomorrow we will speak to Arken."

But Darius did not have time to complain. After everyone had assembled for the evening meal Nemroz asked Arken if the three of them could join him next morning in his quarters.

"Certainly, when I have finished helping Garetta." As Arken was now carrying the pail when Garetta had finished the milking.

Nemroz thanked him and took the meal up to Arlaya. After they had eaten Arlaya said, "I am feeling a little better now. Tomorrow I will go down and tell the family what we are calling our son."

Nemroz smiled with delight and reached towards her.

"Please wait till tomorrow darling, that is the traditional time when you would return to me."

Nemroz turned away and stifled a sob.

Next morning Arlaya asked, "Please can you fetch the breakfasts and ask Garetta and Terrace to come up."

After breakfast they joined them, looking disapprovingly at Nemroz. But he refused to take the hint and stayed. Arrangements were made with the girls that Arlaya would bring the baby down and present him to the family. "Does that include me?" Nemroz asked.

Terrace answered, "You are an outsider."

"But he is the father." Arlaya protested.

The girls just shrugged. Without saying another word, Nemroz stood and left.

Nemroz collected Polto and Darius and they waited for Arken in his room.

"I am sorry we got here first. I hope you didn't mind."

"Not at all. Now what do you want to know?"

"You were telling us about your god."

"Indeed. But I am not sure you believed what I said."

"It is not me you need to convince. My friends were badly hurt in the city. It is hard for them to believe your god loves them."

"What am I supposed to say to convince them?"

"That they are accepted as one of us and that they are as loved as anyone else."

Arken stood stunned. Nemroz continued, "I am keen to hear more, but only if you accept my friends."

"How can you care so much for them?"

"Because they were fellow priests, they are fellow human beings and especially Darius is a wonderful person."

Darius looked away with tears in his eyes.

"You have not really given me chance to explain about our Lord. I am sure He would care for your friends, as He would about anyone else."

"You had better tell us about this lord. Who is he?"

"I think I explained before who God is, that He wants a relationship with all human beings, and He wants them to obey and to rely on Him. But sadly the original human beings did not do that. God had a plan to put things right and restore that relationship. The consequence of that original disobedience was death. The only way for that to be put right was for someone who was not flawed by that disobedience to die. There is no human being on this earth who comes up to that standard. So God came to the earth in person to fulfil that role. That is the Lord. He lived a life on this earth as a human being, without once disobeying any of the laws or instructions. Having achieved that, He died in our place. Does all that make sense to you?"

"These ideas are all very new to us. But the one thing I still want to ask more than any other is. Does all this apply to any and all human beings?"

"Yes as long as they believe who the Lord is, and accept what He did for us."

"I will need to discuss these things with my friends. I am only prepared to proceed if they are willing to proceed."

"That is very loyal of you, but you need to consider yourself. Your life depends on it."

"We will discuss it." And the three of them left.

They went back to the barn. "Can we sit here and talk? Please tell me what you think of what Arken said."

Darius looked shy and said, "Thank you for standing up for us."

Even Polto said, "He seems kinder than the priest in the city. But I am not sure about his god. He seems very different to ours."

I not argue, but in what way?" He was not prepared to say any more.

Darius added, "He still did not say much about our situation. I still do not feel very safe."

Nemroz left it there for the time being and said, "I will see you for the evening meal later."

He returned to the cottage. There were only a few maids in the kitchen. When Nemroz asked where Arlaya was, he was told she was back in their room. He climbed quietly up to the room. Both Arlaya and the baby were asleep. Nemroz slipped quietly in beside her, not wanting to wake her. It was nearly time for the meal by the time she woke.

Nemroz softly asked, "Did you tell the family the name of our son?"

"Yes, but you left."

"Your family did not want me to stay." Nemroz said turning away and feeling very hurt.

"I did not want you to leave."

Nemroz turned to hug her, but she pulled away saying, "Later darling. Please fetch our meals."

Nemroz went back down to fetch their meals, but by the time he returned, Roz was awake and crying for his feed. Nemroz put Arlaya's on the trunk and ate his in silence. Arlaya fed Roz but she could not get him to settle afterwards.

Nemroz said, "I thought I could lie with you once you had been downstairs, but Arlaya did not answer.

Then Nemroz did something he thought he would never do now he had Arlaya. He ran from the room, and as Polto and Darius had left the kitchen, he ran to the barn. He climbed the ladder and quietly crossed the gallery. He crept in beside Darius, who turned over looking surprised. He looked Nemroz up and down and asked, "Are you going to come to me as High Priest?"

"May I?"

"Of course, I am always available for my master."

Nemroz tore off his clothes. Darius lay there ready for him. It was not until Nemroz had calmed down that he realized that Darius was sobbing.

"My dear friend what is wrong? Did you not want me to come to you?"

"You are my master, I am always available for you. When you come to me, I would never stop you. But when I needed you to protect me you sent me away."

"Oh, my dear friend, I never wanted to hurt you. If it had been down to me I would have gladly let you stay. But women have different sensibilities.

When they woke next morning Nemroz was ashamed he had stayed all night. Quickly he dressed and rushed just as he was to the kitchen. He was sad to find Arlaya was already down. He looked around saying, "Where is little Roz?"

"You did not care about that last night."

"I am so sorry, please forgive me. You asked too much of me."

"Eat your breakfast, we will talk up in the room."

"My darling please forgive me."

Arlaya ate in silence and went straight up to the room. "It's all right Terrace I will stay with the baby. I will see you later."

Nemroz rushed up after her, worried what he had done.

Arlaya was sitting on the bed crying. Nemroz sat beside her saying, "Please do not cry, you will have me crying, and you don't like that do you?"

Arlaya sobbed, "How could you?"

"Please forgive me, any man has a breaking point."

"Do you think I enjoyed being like this?"

"All you had to do was talk to me."

She swung round and threw her arms round him. And they fell back on the bed together. They just lay in each other's arms. Then Roz began to cry. Though having a son was an experience he thought he would never have, he was beginning to realize it would mean he would have no time to be with Arlaya alone. Instead of picking up baby Roz, he turned away and shook with silent sobs.

When the baby was quietly suckling, Nemroz turned to Arlaya with longing eyes, "Is there any way someone could look after little Roz, I desperately need to talk to you."

"I am not sure that is how things work."

"Darling this is breaking me. Do you not care?"

"Tonight when Roz has settled I will lie with you. Is that what you want?"

"More than anything, but I also need to talk to you."

"All right you go to the field and come to me later."

By the time Nemroz got back to the kitchen Polto and Darius had gone. Nemroz felt life was falling apart. Not sure what came over him he went to the cow shed to see if Garetta and Arken were still there.

They were astounded to see Nemroz. He turned to Arken saying, "Can I talk to you?"

"When I have finished carrying the pail for Garetta. Please wait for me in my room."

Nemroz went to Arken's room, and sat on the floor. Feeling lost and alone. When Arken came, he sat beside him.

"What is wrong?"

Nemroz started nervously, "Most of this I should not be talking to you about, but I desperately need someone to talk to."

"I am flattered that you found me to talk to. I will never repeat anything that you say. Now what is wrong?"

It all just tumbled out of him. He told Arken about not being able to lie with Arlaya and not being able to talk to her.

"There is something else that is troubling you isn't there?"

"I promised I would never talk to anyone about that, especially not you."

"That is about your friends isn't it?"

Nemroz looked shocked. He said about being with them last night.

"I didn't think you were like that."

"I am not like them, but I desperately needed to be with someone. Now I am terrified I have wrecked my relationship with Arlaya."

"All I can do is be a listening ear. I have never had a woman, let alone a baby."

Nemroz admitted at one time he was not allowed to have a woman of his own. He never believed he could have the love of a woman, and he did not believe it was possible that he could make a son.

Arken was curious, so Nemroz told him about his time at the temple. Arken was beginning to wonder how he could cope with a pagan priest and two homosexuals.

Eventually he said, "I cannot advise you about any of this, but I know what it is like to have no one to share with."

Nemroz gazed at him, "I am sorry I misjudged you. We must speak again. Please never speak of this conversation to Polto or Darius."

"I promise, but is there not someone who could speak to Arlaya for you?"

Though the conversation had found no answers, it had been a great comfort to have someone to talk to. He then turned and left.

Nemroz returned to their room. He was delighted, Arlaya was sitting waiting for him, "My darling please forgive me."

"Yes if you tell me what you were doing last night."

"I am so sorry, I so needed to be with you and to talk to you."

"I cannot always be at your beck and call, now I have a baby. It is hard on me too."

"Will it always be like this now?"

"It will be easier as Roz gets older. Men usually just go away while babies are born."

"I know nothing of your world, there were no fathers with us babies in the temple."

"I do not understand your world either. Garetta would say, that is my fault for marrying a temple priest."

"I am so glad you did. I never thought I could have someone like you." Then he suddenly swung round and kissed her. "Thankyou for talking to me."

"It is nearly time for the evening meal. Can you still bring it to me?"

"Of course I can."

They sat and ate their meal before Roz woke.

"I will need to feed and settle Roz first. Then I don't care what the maids say, I need you. Please wait for me."

"As long as you really need me, I will wait all night. Do you need me to pass Roz to you?"

"I can manage fine. Please take the plates back. But please come back."

"I am sorry I hurt you. Please forgive me. There is no one who could stop me coming straight back."

Nemroz returned, undressed and lay patiently waiting for Arlaya. When Roz was asleep, Arlaya undressed and slid in beside him.

"I do not want to hurt you, you take charge."

"Darling you are wonderful."

"You are well worth waiting for."

When they had finished, Arlaya slid back down beside him.

Nemroz kissed her and said, "I am sorry I got impatient. Can you ever forgive me?"

"I know it was not because you no longer want me. No one could ever be so gentle."

"Darling I love you so much. Please never leave me."

"Neither of us could live without you."

"Me with a son." Nemroz murmured under his breath.

CHAPTER

11

Next morning Nemroz asked, "What would a man from your world do now?"

"He would work in the field by day. The older women say it is still too soon for you to come to me, but please come to me with the evening meal."

"My darling I was so pleased you wanted me."

"I am not sure I can manage that every night yet, but that is not because I don't want you, I love you so much."

"I do not understand, but if you still love me…" he left and fetched breakfast. While he was in the kitchen he asked, Polto, Darius and Arken to wait in the kitchen until he came back.

After breakfast Nemroz asked Arlaya to please take care, and that he would come with the evening meal. He then returned to the kitchen. He went first to Arken to ask if he would join in with helping in the field.

Polto heard, "No way, I am not working with one of them."

"Why?"

"Because he has not assured me that his opinion of us is not the same as that of the priest in the city."

Arken answered saying, "Let me work with you so that I can form an opinion of you both."

Nemroz added, "That seems reasonable enough."

Darius said, "As long as you will be there sir. I am willing to give it a try."

"I appreciate that. You can call me Nemroz you know."

Darius just grinned. But Polto was still very reluctant.

So Nemroz just joked, "You're just lazy Polto."

So he replied, "I'll help Garetta." And walked off.

So Nemroz, Darius and Arken set out for the barn to collect the tools. Nemroz spent the day showing Arken what needed to be done. On the way back Arken said, "It has been tiring and I ache, but it has been great working with other people. Thankyou Nemroz for rescuing me." And to Darius he said, "I hope you will learn to trust me."

Nemroz left asking Darius what he thought until they were alone.

Nemroz cleaned up, then collected the meal and went up to Arlaya, She asked, "How did the day go?"

"It was not going to be easy to get Polto and Darius to work with Arken. Darius gave it a try, but Polto didn't."

"Oh, Arken seemed alright to me."

"And how are you?"

"Roz is getting into a bit of a routine now. But." And she stopped.

"Darling what is wrong?"

"I don't feel up to..." she hesitated.

"Being intimate." Nemroz prompted.

"Yes, you remember before we were first married, you just pressed up against me. Would you like to do that again?"

"That is kind. I would rather be fully married, but if you are really not up to it, I would be satisfied with that."

"Darling you are wonderful."

So when they were settled that is what they did.

For several days Arken willingly joined Nemroz and Darius in the field. But then one morning after breakfast he announced that his God required him to dedicate one day in seven just to worshiping Him, and said, "If you wish to join me in my room, you are welcome."

"Who's lazy now?" Polto snorted, and he walked off.

Nemroz and Darius looked a little stunned, and left for the barn. When inside Nemroz took the opportunity to speak to Darius, "How are things with Polto these days?"

"You know I always prefer to be with Polto, but I am worried about his attitude over, (canI call him Arken?)"

"I am sure Arken is fine. What is wrong with Polto?"

"He says he thinks, Arken is against our relationship, like the city priest was."

"Arken has not said so."

"But he hasn't said he isn't either."

"And what do you think of Arken?"

"He seems nice."

"And what do you think of what Arken says about his god?"

"Polto does not let me say."

"Polto isn't here and I am asking you what you think."

Darius threw his arms round Nemroz. When he had composed himself he said, "I like the sound of him, but I am still not sure we are acceptable."

"Would you like to go to Arken's room. We could ask him?"

"Polto would be furious. I am scared he would hurt me again."

"My dear Darius it is not right that you should be with Polto if you are still scared of him."

"But what can I do? I could not live without him."

"I can never understand why you love Polto so much."

"I have always loved Polto, it is like he is part of me."

"But you need to be able to make up your own mind about things."

"I am not strong like you. I have always been pushed around, since I was a young boy."

"I wish I had known you then, I would have stood up for you."

"I wish I could just love you, but there are so many reasons why that will never happen."

"What should we do this morning?"

"If you want to go to Arken, we should go."

"But what about Polto."

"Don't worry about me. I will stay with Polto even if he will kill me." He said no more. He held out his hand and opened the door.

Nemroz was pleased he took the lead, but it reminded him of the time when he did that in the temple. But as they crossed the yard to the servants' quarters Darius was less sure.

They entered and found their way back to Arken's room. Nemroz knocked on the door and was reassured by Arken's voice calling, "Come in."

As they entered Arken moved to the floor and the other two joined him.

Arken said, "So far I have only been praying. Did your work in the temple include praying?"

"What is praying?" Nemroz asked

"Basically it is talking to the deity."

"We would not presume to talk to ours." Said Nemroz rather puzzled.

"That is where our God is very different. He wants a relationship with us."

To everyone's surprise it was Darius who replied, "Even me?"

"Yes, even you."

And Arken was even more surprised when Darius fell at his feet. Arken was taken aback, but he said, "Come, do not bow down to me."

"But you do not have a statue of your god."

Arken was quite overcome, but eventually he responded with, "Do you believe in what I was saying the other day?"

And they were both more surprised still when Darius replied, "Yes, if your god will accept even me."

Then Darius realized what danger that would probably put him in, and he collapsed in tears. Arken looked very concerned. "My dear fellow. What is the matter?"

Darius looked imploringly at Nemroz. "You promised you would not tell about me and Polto. I should go. He will kill me."

Darius went to run, but before he could stand Nemroz threw his arms round him.

"Wait Darius, now you have come this far it would be safer to tell Arken what this is all about. If you don't I will."

"But you promised."

"You tell him then."

Darius sat back down and sobbed.

Feeling bewildered Arken turned to Nemroz, "What have I done?"

"Darius has a conflict. He should tell you himself. Perhaps we should go."

"Please do not leave like this. Just stay. I will not say anymore."

Darius relaxed, but he was still weeping. After a while he sobbed. "This isn't right I shouldn't be telling you of all people. He will kill me."

"Are you exaggerating? Or is there really someone who will hurt you?"

"It does not matter what he does."

That got Arken really worried, he began to guess what was happening. Dare he ask? He looked anxiously at Nemroz and whispered, "Is it Polto?"

Arken gently took Darius by the hand and said, "I think you ought to tell me all about it."

"I can't."

"Does Nemroz know about it?"

Darius sobbed all the more, and slightly nodded.

"Can he tell me?" Nemroz rushed to his side.

"No, you promised."

"I am sure Arken will help."

"He is the last person who can help."

Arken calmly said, "Give me the chance to try. I hate to see you distraught like this."

"You care?"

"Yes, I care."

Darius collapsed into Arken's lap and tried to tell Arken the whole story. And Nemroz helped. Arken had never had to deal with anything like this, and he was lost for words.

Eventually he said, "I don't think he should be with Polto."

Darius tried to jump up, yelling, "Don't take me away from him. I couldn't survive that. I would rather Polto killed me."

In spite of Darius's size it took both of them to hold him down. Nemroz tried hard to remember enough words in Arken's language. He managed to say. "I will fetch him. Keep Darius here."

Arken had to pin Darius to the floor for Nemroz to leave.

At first Nemroz could not find Polto. But when he eventually found him he said. "Darius is in trouble, he needs you."

At first Polto glared at Nemroz. Then when he said, "Do you not have any feeling left for Darius?"

He reluctantly followed. When he realized where they were going he said, "I am not going to see Arken."

But Nemroz replied, "Darius is in distress. Are you going to desert him?"

Polto was not happy. By the time they entered Arken's room Darius had calmed down a little. He was just leaning against the wall. When he saw Polto he rushed to his side.

Arken turned to him and said, "I forced your friend to tell me about the injuries he had a while ago."

"How dare you. What did he tell you?" he replied, glaring at Darius. Who was trembling and gazing imploringly at Polto.

"He told us eventually that you beat him."

"He deserved it."

"All I have ever done is love you." Darius sobbed

"Be quiet!" Polto growled.

"It's alright, we know about your relationship with Darius."

Darius collapsed at Polto's feet. "You fool!" he growled. Kicking him away.

Darius looked up at him and pleaded, "Are you going to beat me again?"

"You wimp." Polto snapped, and turned to leave. But Nemroz barred his way.

"To think I used to like you once, when we were friends at the temple."

Polto stopped short, and he looked as though he was not far from tears.

Arken said, still in a quiet, calm voice, "Why don't you tell us what all this is about."

"All what?"

"All this rage aimed at your poor friend."

Polto thought for a moment looking first Nemroz then Arken up and down. "That is what Darius is for."

A puzzled Darius said, "For you to repay love with beatings. I don't understand. Why can't you love me?"

Arken said, "Do you think it is fair or kind, to repay love with beatings?"

"He will get both of us beatings with stupid talk like that."

"There is no one here that will beat you."

"Only your believers." Polto growled.

"I do not have any believers."

"Oh yes?"

Nemroz added, "Polto that is why we left the city. This is not the city."

"I don't believe you, any of you."

Darius was weeping, "Please help him he has gone mad."

Arken showed everyone but Polto out of the room and shut Polto in.

He said, "Sadly Darius is right, Polto is out of his mind. I know all Darius wants is to be with Polto, but sadly that just isn't safe. I realize it is punishing Darius, but he must not be allowed to be with him for now."

"No. No I will die anyway if you keep us apart."

Nemroz added, "Believe me I understand how much this means to you. But remember you survived when Polto gave you to me. And you will be with me all day."

"But where will I be at night? In the temple I was always with you at night."

"You could stay with me." Arken suggested.

"How could I? You do not understand me."

"Give it a try. You would be safe with me."

"Nemroz, sir, please help me."

"Please stay with Arken for now. I would hate anything to happen to you."

"But not enough for you to let me be with you."

"Now that is not fair."

Darius ran off in tears.

Nemroz said to Arken. "Leave him, I will get him to come to you. Thankyou for the offer. Where would be the safest place to keep Polto?"

"I think we should ask Pops."

Darius stepped in front of Nemroz, imploring him, "You know I would do anything for Polto, but can I see you first?"

Surprised that for once Darius asked for something for himself, Nemroz took his hand and led him to the barn. Once they were inside Darius sobbed, "I am sorry it is not for me to ask you, but will you let me come to you? I need you so."

When Nemroz did not resist, he ran to the ladder, to the back of the gallery.

"I am sorry my master. Can I?"

Before Nemroz had even undone the first fastening, Darius was undressed.

"Forgive me for asking, this is tearing me apart."

By the time Nemroz lay with him. He was almost frantic.

"I am sorry, please forgive. My master forgive me."

Nemroz was too heartbroken to answer.

When he had finished, he sobbed, "Thankyou, my master, thankyou. Would it be wrong to ask one thing more? Will you come to me?"

As Nemroz turned over, Darius reached to him, to help as he had done in the temple. When Nemroz was ready he turned Darius over.

When Darius calmed down, Nemroz said to him, "It is wonderful that you ask for something for yourself."

"You were not cross?"

"How could I be, you always give, but you never take."

"Oh, my master, why can't Polto love me like that? All I can ever remember is wanting Polto to need me and want me."

Nemroz replied, "Time is getting on. We should go and find Pops."

"Yes of course, please forgive me for wanting you first." He dressed and descended the ladder without another word. When he reached the door he held it open for Nemroz.

They crossed the yard and entered the kitchen. Pops was already there, even though the maids had not even started laying things ready for the meal yet. Nemroz sat by the elderly man. He scowled at the seat. Nemroz said gently, "I will return to my seat for the meal, I need to speak to you sir."

"Well what do you want?"

He thought, 'There is no point in messing about.' So he stated, "We are having trouble with Polto. We need somewhere safe and secure to keep him."

"All you priests are trouble. What kind of somewhere do you need?"

"Somewhere simple we can hold shut from the outside."

"A prison?" said the old man coldly. And Nemroz winced.

Pops thought for a moment, then said, "There is a little space round the back of the servants' quarters that you could use, but it would need to be cleaned out."

"Many thanks sir. Come Darius let us see." They left to investigate. They found the space they were told of, but it was in an awful state.

"We can't put Polto in there." Darius protested.

"We will clean it out. Then it is up to him. He is not safe to be let loose."

"Please, please." Darius begged, "Do not do this to him."

They went back to see Arken. He was still sitting against his door. Nemroz apologised to Arken for being so long, (without explaining). Then said, "We have a place for Polto, but it will need a lot of cleaning, we will not have it ready for tonight. Is there a way we can barricade him in your room for now?" They managed to secure the door, and they went to the kitchen for their meal. With Darius protesting all the way.

By the time they returned to the kitchen, Arlaya was there with Roz. Nemroz turned to her, a worried look on his face saying, "We have a problem, Polto has gone completely mad. Pops has given us a place to keep him, but it will have to be cleaned out and we cannot get it done by tonight."

Arken chipped in "I can keep Polto safe tonight, but we have nowhere safe for Darius to sleep."

She replied, "He is not sleeping in with us, that is not right."

Poor Darius first just sat quietly sobbing, then he cried out, "Please do not throw me out on my own. None of this is my fault."

Everyone, even Pops looked round with compassion. Pops said, "He can sleep on the floor in my room, just for tonight."

Darius was so astonished he gasped, "Thankyou very much sir."

As soon as they had finished their meal, Arken hurried back to his room, he was relieved to find Polto had not attempted to break out. He had brought some food for Polto, but he refused to eat any, but he did drink some milk. Arken slept against the outside of his door. Darius slept on the floor in Pops's bedroom. Only Nemroz and Arlaya had their normal bed.

When they were settled in bed Nemroz said, "I am so worried about Polto, I do not know what has made him like this. I feel it is cruel to lock him up. But I am scared, no one is safe. And poor Darius is distraught. How will he survive this?"

"They are not your responsibility."

"But I feel they are."

"Darling, forget them and come to me."

"I am so lucky, it is so unfair."

"There is no reason why you should not be happy. Denying yourself will not make things right for Darius and Polto. I am sure you will do your best tomorrow."

"Oh, Arlaya I want You."

Next morning all three of them went to the little room round the back of the servants' quarters. They worked all day to get it clean. By the end of the day it was useable.

Darius pleaded, "Can I go to Polto?"

"Not on your own."

"Then you come with me." He begged.

All three went round to Arken's room. They removed the barricade and Darius rushed in. Polto was lying on Arken's bed looking very subdued. Darius rushed up to him and fell on his knees by the bed.

"Oh my darling, I do not agree with what they are doing to you. Why can't you just love me?"

Polto just lay there staring blankly at the ceiling.

Arken said, "Polto has more need of a bed. We should take the mattress for him."

Nemroz lifted him from the bed. Arken took him by the arm and Nemroz carried the mattress. Darius threw himself on the floor by the wall and howled.

Nemroz laid the mattress on the floor in the little room and gently laid Polto on it. "I wish I could make you better. I hope you will not be too unhappy. I will come in the morning."

They quietly left and locked Polto in.

Nemroz walked back to Arken's room with him. "Will Darius be alright with you? Be gentle with him. All this is upsetting him dreadfully."

"Darius will be fine. You go to Arlaya."

"You are kind. I do not expect you to understand Polto and Darius."

"Trust me I will be gentle."

When Arken entered his room, Darius was just lying on the floor whimpering. When Arken lay beside him, he spluttered, "No, please go... I just... You don't approve."

"I hate to see you so upset."

"You can't help. Please go away."

Arken was sad, but he left him and slept on the floor on the other side of the room.

Next morning Darius did not wait for Arken he rushed to the cottage. He would not speak to anyone. But as soon as Nemroz appeared he rushed to his side. "I want to take something to Polto, but Arken said I cannot go alone."

"Why could you not go with Arken?

"You know I cannot do that. Can you come with me?"

"You have your breakfast. Then we will go."

He sadly sat down, but he could not eat anything. Just drank a little milk.

When Nemroz had finished Darius said, "Can we go now? You can take some breakfast if you like, but I am sure he will only have milk."

Nemroz stood saying to Arlaya, "I will see you later." And they headed for Polto's little cell.

On the way Darius said, "I want to lie with Polto if he wants me. I could not do that with Arken there, he does not approve. Being with Arken is going to be very hard."

"Be brave, you know I will not stop you. But be careful that Polto wants you."

"Why can't Polto just love me? I love him so much."

Nemroz opened up the door and Darius rushed in and knelt by the mattress where Polto still lay staring blankly at the ceiling.

"Oh my dear Polto, I have brought you some milk." He gently raised Polto's head. Slowly some focus came into Polto's eyes. He sipped at the milk, then said, "Is that you Darius?"

"Yes my dear, it's me."

"I didn't think you would come again."

"Of course I will come to you. I cannot live without you."

Polto helplessly held out his arms to him, "Please come to me."

"Do you really want me?" Darius said with a beaming smile of delight.

"Can you help me?"

Darius oh so gently removed Polto's lower garments, then hurriedly removed his own, and lay on the mattress beside him. Polto's attempts were very weak but Darius was very gentle and patient with him.

When they had finished Nemroz said gently, "We should go to the field."

"Yes, you go to the field. I am sorry to disobey you, but I cannot come. You go I will be alright."

Polto answered weakly, "I will not hurt him."

Darius gazed at him, "Thankyou for wanting me, I will not let him make me leave you."

Nemroz had known Darius's desire for Polto before, but this was a new intensity. He sat at the end of the mattress and gave a resigned sigh.

"Why can't you understand all I have ever wanted is for you to want me. Can I come to you?"

Polto reached out and touched him, then rolled over.

"There is no need for you to stay."

"If anything happens to you, I would never forgive myself."

"Please Darius." Polto sobbed.

Darius had great difficulty kerbing his enthusiasm. When Darius withdrew, Polto weakly looked up at Nemroz, "Will you ever be able to trust me again?"

Darius answered, "I will always trust you, what ever you do."

"I don't understand what has happened to me. But I know I do not deserve you."

"Nemroz the maids need the vegetables, but Polto needs me."

"How ever ill you are, if you hurt Darius I will kill you, however much that will hurt Darius."

"I am sure Polto will not hurt me again. But if he does, you must kill me too."

Nemroz was tormented, but he left.

Nemroz worked in the field, but his mind was elsewhere.

Arken worked with the girls and the maids. When they found that Arken and Darius had slept on the floor they found an old featherbed that had been stowed away, and between them they got it to Arken's room. Darius had spent the whole day with Polto, so he knew nothing about it.

When it was drawing towards the evening Darius asked Polto if he could bring him a meal. Polto insisted he could not eat a meal.

"In the city you managed broth. I will get the maids to make some broth."

Polto agreed.

Darius tried the door. Nemroz had not locked it.

"If I try to get the maids to make some broth, promise me you will not try to leave."

"If you promise to come back to me."

"I will not let them stop me. Stay safe my darling."

Darius hurried to the kitchen. He persuaded one of the maids to boil some vegetables and make some thin broth. By the time it was ready Nemroz and Arken had returned. But Darius insisted he took some broth and some milk to Polto before he had anything himself. He helped Polto just as he had in the city.

"I must go now. Will you be alright?"

"Darius you are so good to me."

"I will not be able to stay with you at night. Would you be happier if you are not shut in?"

"Will you get into trouble?"

"That will not matter. Would you be happier? But if you escape I will not be able to come to you again."

"How can I get better if you do not come to me?"

"You behave then, and I will come to you as soon as I can."

Darius went back to the kitchen, but he persuaded Nemroz not to tell anyone that he had been with Polto all day. Arken took him to his room again. On entering Darius stared at the featherbed. He looked around and when he realized there was no other bed he cried, "You cannot expect me to sleep with you on that."

Arken looked surprised, "Why not?"

"When I am asleep I would put my arms round you, and you would not approve of that."

Arken looked very uncomfortable.

"You do not understand Polto and me."

Arken sat on the edge of the bare bed and fidgeted.

"You are not like Polto and me, and your god says we are wrong."

Arken was getting more and more embarrassed.

Darius was surprising himself, but having started he continued, "This will not work. Nemroz has Arlaya. I will lie with Polto."

Very alarmed Arken cried, "You cannot do that!"

"I have been with Polto most of the day. He has not hurt me."

He went to leave, but Arken stopped him.

"If I sleep on that, I can't promise not to put my arms round you when I am asleep."

"You sleep on the, (what did the maids call it?). I will sleep on the floor."

"I cannot expect you to do that."

"Well you are not to go to Polto."

"I will sleep on the floor then. This is your room." They agreed on that.

Darius lay on the floor by the wall as he had the night before. But as soon as he was sufficiently sure that Arken was asleep, he crept out and round to Polto's little cell. He undressed and slipped in beside him. Polto woke alarmed at first.

"It's all right, it is only me."

A sleepy Polto said, "Is that you Darius? You frightened me."

"I am sorry, do not be frightened of me. Do you want me to come?"

"Oh my darling, I am so glad you are here. I hate being on my own."

"I am so glad you want me here. I so much prefer to be with you. Please go back to sleep, I didn't mean to wake you. You need your sleep."

He turned over and threw his arms round his friend. Darius now happy went to sleep.

They slept happily in each other's arms for several hours. When Polto woke he was delighted to find Darius was still there, and gave him a kiss. Darius woke with a start.

"Good morning, you didn't try to go out did you?"

"Only to wee outside. It is nice not to be locked in. Please don't let them do that again."

"I didn't want you locked in. They will not listen to me. I cannot stay with you all day again today. Do you want me to come to you before the others get up?"

Polto reach down for him and he readily responded. Polto turned over, quivering with anticipation. Darius was too excited to show restraint this time. He had only just begun when Arken came bursting through the door. He stopped dead and gasped. Darius found it difficult to stop. Then he burst into tears. Polto just didn't move. Darius was too worried to turn over.

After a few moments Arken recovered enough to say, "I told you not to come to Polto."

Still without turning over Darius replied, "Polto needs loving for him to get better."

But Arken replied as calmly as he could muster, "Is that what you do when you are together?"

"Nemroz doesn't mind."

"My God does."

"We do not belong to your god. And if he cannot accept us as we are, Nemroz is welcome to your god."

Arken was so shocked he did not know what to say. He could not stop himself saying, "This is disgusting." Then he turned saying, "I will see if they are awake in the cottage."

As Polto turned to Darius, Darius was surprised to see that he was looking scared. Polto whispered, "What will they do to me?"

"I will not let them hurt you. I will make them listen." Then he muttered, more to reassure himself, "We are not in the city now."

Eventually Arken returned with Nemroz, who stood over Darius, glaring down at him, "This behaviour is not acceptable. If Arken told you to stay with him, you should not be here. And you should never answer Arken back like that. I don't know what has come over you."

"Arken is not my master. And I think you are both being very cruel to Polto."

Nemroz stared at Darius aghast. "I don't know what has come over you."

Surprised at himself Darius continued, "I can't sit back and let you treat Polto like this."

"Darius you are not safe."

"I am prepared to take that risk, that is up to me. I am not prepared to let you lock him up, he could not even relieve himself."

Arken and Nemroz were too shocked to reply.

Eventually Nemroz said, "Go to breakfast, and never speak to me like that."

With a direct order from Nemroz, Darius wavered. He clung to Polto.

Then he sobbed, "Please don't lock him up on his own, he was so unhappy."

Nemroz was furious, he turned to Arken saying, "We must go to breakfast." And stormed out. Arken followed. An astounded Polto dissolved into tears.

Darius just sat trembling. "I should fetch you some breakfast. Could you manage to eat a little?"

"You know when I am upset it would not stay down."

"Oh my darling they must let me help you. I made you better before, if they let me I could make you better again."

"But we had Nemroz on our side then."

"I can't believe Nemroz does not want you to get better. I am going for some milk. You would not try to go out would you?"

"Can I come with you?"

"It would be safer for you to stay here. I will come straight back."

Darius went straight to one of the maids and asked for two beakers of milk. Before anyone had time to stop him he was gone.

"My dear Darius I don't deserve you."

"Just let me love you. That is all I have ever asked."

"Forgive me, I have so often let you down."

"Please drink your milk. Let me make you better again."

"I don't know that you can this time. Some days I cannot control what I do."

"I know. Can I ask you something?"

"What do you want to know?"

"What would you do if you killed me?"

Polto collapsed into sobs. Between sobs he gasped, "Never let me do that."

"I don't know I can this time."

"Forgive me. What would I do without you."

"Do you mean that?"

111

"Why have I never seen that before?"

Darius fell at his feet sobbing, I will die happy." He gasped and collapsed. Polto threw his arms round Darius crying, "What has happened, what is the matter with you?" He took him up in his arms, "My darling speak to me. You did not really mean that you would die?" I have not hurt you, I need you so much."

At that moment Nemroz came bursting back in. Polto wailed, "Please help Darius, I do not know what is the matter with him."

Nemroz took Darius in his arms shouting, "What have you done to him?"

"I have not hurt him. Please believe me I have not hurt him."

"You must have done something."

"I only said I needed him."

As Nemroz rushed out in the fresh air with him in his arms he replied, "Darius has longed to hear that from you, it has overwhelmed him."

When Polto tried to follow, Nemroz roared, "You stay where you are."

"Nemroz please do not take Darius away from me. I beg you please."

"A bit late to think of that now. Stay and drink your milk."

Nemroz lay down outside with Darius on top of him, the way he had in the city. In a while he regained consciousness. Nemroz gasped with relief.

In an unsteady voice Darius asked, "Where is Polto?"

Nemroz replied, "What did he do to you?"

"He did not hurt me. What happened?"

"You passed out. He must have hurt you."

"I assure you he didn't. I am not hurt. Did you send him away?"

"I took you outside for some air."

"Where is Polto, has he left me?" and he burst into tears. From inside Polto could hear what was said and he rushed to Darius weeping, "I have not left you. Nemroz took you away from me. Please Nemroz let me hold him. Please trust me I will not hurt him."

"Why does no one let us be together? All my life the one thing I have wanted was for Polto to want me, for just me. He says he really wants me and you take me away from him."

"Darius forgive me. Why has it taken so long for me to realize you are the most wonderful person in the world?"

"My master please let him hold me, if you have ever cared for either of us."

Reluctantly Nemroz handed Darius into Polto's arms. He held him so gently.

"Did you really mean that? I never thought I would hear you say something like that. I thought you letting me love you was the best I could ever hope for in life."

Polto pleaded, "Is there somewhere I can take him? We can make each other well."

They had not realized Arken had been listening. "Take them to my room. I have seen why they need to be together."

Arken helped Polto and Nemroz carried Darius. They laid them on the featherbed.

"I am not happy about what you do, but I can see it grows out of true love. I have never seen such devotion as Darius has for Polto, it puts a lot of married couples to shame."

"Never let them take you away from me again. I would kill myself before I would harm you again. Please forgive me."

"I would forgive you anything if you love me. Please never leave me."

Nemroz said to Arken, "Come we should let them rest."

"But they…"

"Will you come and help me in the field. I am struggling to do it all on my own." While walking to the field Nemroz asked, "If your god is a god of love, why can he not accept people like Darius? No one loves more than Darius."

"He certainly is unusual."

"Darius is unique. I am so glad Polto is beginning to appreciate him at long last."

"It is just what they do when they are together…"

"That was quite normal in the temple. Even for those who are not like Polto and Darius. We all did it, we were not allowed to have women in the temple."

Arken looked shocked, "Did you do that?"

"With Darius yes. Will you reject us because of that?"

"You have Arlaya now."

"Yes, but the other two would never take a woman."

"I suppose they will never stop doing such things."

"Surely you could not be so cruel after all Darius has been through."

"Sin is sin."

"I do not understand why he could accept me but not Darius."

"I will ask for a sign. If God accepts them, it is not for me to reject them."

Nemroz left it at that. They collected the tools and went to the field.

They worked for several hours, until Arken was beginning to tire.

"Come, that will do for today."

They returned the tools to the barn and took the vegetables to the kitchen.

"Before it is time for the evening meal, let us go to see the others."

As they quietly entered Arken's room, Polto and Darius were asleep in each other's arms.

Darius opened his eyes and looked up sleepily, "Is that you Nemroz?"

"Yes it's me. How are you feeling now?"

"I will be okay. You haven't come to take Polto away have you?"

"No, we have agreed to give him another chance."

"Oh, thankyou so much. Can we stay together?"

"Are you sure you are safe?"

"I have always told you, I would stay with Polto what ever he does. But I really do think he would not hurt me again."

Polto rolled over saying, "Please trust me, I would never hurt him again."

"You have said that before."

"If I went crazy again, I would kill myself to save you the trouble."

"No, Polto no!"

"Its okay, I am sure you will make me well again, like you did in the city."

He cringed and turned away at the thought of the city.

"It's alright it will never be like that again."

"Can you two manage a meal?"

Darius looked at Polto, "What do you think?"

"I dare not try more than a broth."

"I will go and see the maid again." to Nemroz, "Can Polto come with me?"

"Do you feel strong enough Polto?"

"If Darius will help me."

"Darius is not strong either. Lean on me. Darius can lean on Arken."

Darius looked nervously at Arken, who replied, "It's alright, I am beginning to understand you now."

Darius looked puzzled, but he took Arken's arm. The four of them returned to the kitchen.

Darius asked Nemroz if they could sit at the table. When Arlaya joined them she said to Nemroz, "I need to talk to you."

"I need to go to Arken's room with the others, but I will come to our room as soon as I can."

Polto managed some vegetable broth and Darius had a small portion of the meal.

When they had finished eating, the four of them went to Arken's room.

Nemroz started, "I have been asking Arken more about his god."

Polto looked apprehensive.

"It's alright, he is not going to chide you. Their culture is different to ours, but surely love is love. If you are willing, we will learn more about this god of love. If he does not reject you. I am keen to learn how to respond to him."

It was Darius who said, "Is he likely to accept us?"

Nemroz looked to Arken. "Especially Darius is a special human being. I cannot see that anyone could reject him."

Darius looked amazed. "And Polto?" he asked anxiously.

"If Polto is willing to learn from you, and will in every other respect do as is asked, it is up to God Himself."

"We will come back tomorrow."

"You are kind sir. As long as I can stay with Polto."

Arken slept on the mattress in the cell and Nemroz returned to Arlaya.

CHAPTER

12

To Nemroz's surprise and relief Roz was already fed and settled, and Arlaya was in bed and waiting for him.

"Will your friends always come first?"

"I am sorry, I am here now."

"I have been with the family."

"Why is there something wrong?"

"No not really wrong. The cow needs to be taken each year to my uncle's farm. They have a bull, since the invasion we do not. So our cow has to be taken to their farm to be serviced. Terrace and some of the maids will have to go. If you remember, when you first came you and your friends said you would escort them, as it is a dangerous journey."

"That is difficult at the moment. Polto and Darius are not very strong. And surely you do not expect me to go. I am working on my own much of the time. Who would gather the vegetables if I go?"

"Ask the others tomorrow. We cannot wait for long."

"It is one thing after another, I never get any peace."

"My darling, just relax for now and come to me. What would we have done if you were not here? I hope Pops appreciates that."

As Nemroz relaxed in Arlaya's arms the world melted away.

But in the morning it was back. He woke, Arlaya asked anxiously, "If the cow does not travel to the other farm, what do we do for milk?"

"If we do not take her, will there be no milk? Polto is unwell, he can only take milk."

"Then it is more important that she goes. The journey is already overdue."

"Darling I must go to them."

"If you must. You always sort them out."

Nemroz quickly dressed and crossed to Arken's room. And quietly opened the door and slipped in beside them. As soon as Darius felt Nemroz beside him he woke and turned over.

"My master is there something wrong?"

"Are you awake? I need to talk to you."

Darius blinked and sat up. "What is wrong?"

Nemroz explained about the cow.

"But what will happen to Polto? He is not well enough to keep anything else down again."

"Is there any chance you could be well enough to go with Terrace?"

"We could try, but Polto is not strong enough. He cannot eat."

"But if he does not go there will be no milk for him, and the trip is already overdue."

Darius gently kissed Polto on the back of the neck. He quivered and turned over.

"Please wake up we have a problem." He explained.

Nemroz said, "I will ask Arken to go with you, to help and protect you. Come we must go to breakfast."

They went and washed at the trough and went for breakfast. Arken was already there. As they sat down Nemroz told Arken they needed to talk straight after breakfast. "We will go to your room."

As they left Nemroz said to Arlaya, "I will sort it, I will see you later."

Nemroz explained the situation to Arken and asked him to escort the party.

"I will do anything to help, but is Polto strong enough?"

Nemroz explained, "When Polto was rescued in the city he was in a bad way. No one has been able to get him to tell them what he had been through, not even Darius. It appears to have damaged his insides. If he is badly stressed he cannot keep solid food down. So at the moment, if he is not able to have milk, he will be in trouble. If the cow is taken on her journey, Polto will have no milk. So Polto must go too. Polto was looking away and trembling. Arken asked Nemroz to fetch Terrace.

He returned to the kitchen, where Arlaya was feeding Roz. "Where will I find Terrace?"

"She will be in the cow shed."

"Thankyou, I will see you later." Nemroz hurried to the cow shed, where Terrace had nearly finished the milking. He knelt by her saying. "I will take the pail. As soon as you have taken the cow back to the field, please go to Arken's room. I will join you there."

The priests between them explained the situation and Arken asked details of when they were going, then he said he would see her at the evening meal. Surprised she left.

"There is something I must ask all three of you." They went quiet and looked at Arken. "You said about committing yourselves to the Lord. There is a public ritual to declare your commitment. You are individually dunked in water. Since we will be travelling along the stream that runs between here and the other farm. That will be an ideal opportunity. Are you ready for that commitment?"

They all looked at each other. Then surprisingly it was Darius who answered, "If this lord has gone through so much, and is even willing to accept me. How could I refuse?"

With tears in his eyes, Nemroz answered, "Since the days in the city I have longed to hear you say that."

Then all eyes turned to Polto, "Can I talk to Darius first?"

Nemroz turned to Arken. "Come, we will return shortly."

Outside Arken said, "If you can come with us as far as the stream. You can then return to Arlaya."

After a while they returned to the others. Darius said, "Polto is prepared to go ahead."

"I need to hear that from Polto himself."

"If this lord is willing to accept me too, and will not reject me being with Darius. If that will not alter my relationship with either Darius or Nemroz. I am prepared to commit to him."

Arrangements were made to leave in two days time. Nemroz went with them as far as the stream. All three of them were baptised. Arken, Polto, Darius, Terrace and the maids continued with the cow. And Nemroz returned to Arlaya.

For several days everyone thought all was well. Then when everyone was thinking the party should have arrived at Pops's brother's farm, a much depleted, wounded and bloodstained group struggled into the yard. A terrified Nemroz rushed up to Arken howling "Where are the others?"

Only Arken, Terrace and one of the maids had survived.

CPSIA information can be obtained
at www.ICGtesting.com
Printed in the USA
LVHW040135250322
714345LV00006B/87